LUSITANIA

GHOSTS OF SOUTHAMPTON
BOOK FOUR

ID JOHNSON

For Kate

CONTENTS

Chapter 1 — 1
Chapter 2 — 9
Chapter 3 — 15
Chapter 4 — 23
Chapter 5 — 29
Chapter 6 — 35
Chapter 7 — 41
Chapter 8 — 47
Chapter 9 — 53
Chapter 10 — 59
Chapter 11 — 65
Chapter 12 — 71
Chapter 13 — 77
Chapter 14 — 83
Chapter 15 — 89
Chapter 16 — 95
Chapter 17 — 103
Chapter 18 — 109
Chapter 19 — 115
Chapter 20 — 123
Chapter 21 — 129
Chapter 22 — 135
Chapter 23 — 141
Chapter 24 — 147
Chapter 25 — 153
Chapter 26 — 159
Chapter 27 — 165
Chapter 28 — 171
Chapter 29 — 179
Chapter 30 — 185
Epilogue — 193

A Note From the Author — 197
Also by ID Johnson — 199

1

April 29, 1915

CARRIE BOXHALL SAT on the floor of the nursery in the home of her employers, Charles and Meg Ashton, keeping the children company while Meg and her good friend Kelly O'Connell visited in a nearby parlor. Even though Henry, Meg's son, had a governess, Carrie didn't mind. She often found herself spending time with Henry, Ruth, and Lizzie while Mrs. Pendleton took her tea in the same room as their mistress. It gave the governess a chance to visit with other adults, and it gave Carrie a chance to dream of having her own children, something she'd very much like to experience one day.

Henry, who had just turned two a couple of weeks ago, grabbed for the toy train Ruth was holding in her hand. Ruth, who was seven, told him, "You can't just take things away from other people, Henry. Even if it is your train."

"He's so little," Carrie said with a smile. "He doesn't quite know how to share yet, Miss Ruth."

"Someone should probably teach him," the oldest child of the three replied in no uncertain terms. Her sister, Lizzie, who was three, was busy banging a toy pot with a spoon. Earlier, Carrie had been showing her how to stir it up and taste it, which had Lizzie in a fit of giggles. Now, she was more concerned about making sure Henry didn't start to cry.

"Would you like this train instead, Master Henry?" She pulled a different locomotive out of a large basket full of toys and waved it in front of him. He laughed and bounced up and down a few times before taking it and doing his best to say train.

"He doesn't even know how to talk properly," Ruth said with a sigh.

"I bet you didn't either when you were only two." Carrie smiled at the girl.

"My mother says I was born speaking like a twenty-year-old woman." Ruth pursed her lips together and straightened a lock of her red hair. "I've always been quite intelligent."

Biting back a laugh, Carrie said, "Yes, I suppose that's true."

Just then, Lizzie wandered over to where Ruth had deposited a couple of her dolls earlier. As her sister's hand came down to touch a pink frock, Ruth bolted over to stop her.

"No, Lizzie! Those are mine." Ruth stood between her sister and the dolls.

Lizzie's eyes narrowed, and she jutted out her bottom lip. "Me play whiff them."

"No!" Ruth insisted, gathering them up. "No one touches them but me."

"Would you like for me to put them up on top of the shelf in the bureau so she can't reach them?" Carrie asked, standing to join the girls next to the rocking chair where they were still glaring at one another.

Ruth's eyes trailed up to the highest shelf. "I don't know," she said, rearranging the three dolls in her arms. "Lilac and Charlotte would probably be fine, but Dolly New-Eyes doesn't like to be so far away from me."

"Dolly New-Eyes?" Carrie repeated. She'd seen Ruth carrying around the dolls before but couldn't remember ever hearing their names.

"This one." Ruth held the doll in question out for her to see. The eyes were shiny blue marbles. "It used to be Aunty Meg's when she was a little girl, but the eyes fell out. Daddy put marbles in for me. Uncle Charlie said he could take her to a doll store to get her fixed up good, but she likes her pretty eyes."

"I see." Carrie smiled and bit back a laugh. "Well, perhaps we can put the other two up there, and you can keep a hold of Dolly."

"Dolly New Eyes," Ruth corrected.

"Yes, of course." She reached out for the other two dolls, and Ruth handed them to her with a reluctant sigh. Carrie thanked her and situated the other two dolls out of Lizzie's reach. "That one must be awfully special to you then, since your aunt gave it to you."

"She is special to me, but not because of that." Ruth sat down on the rocking chair and began to rock while Lizzie went back to the toys to find a different doll.

"Oh? Why is she so special then, Miss Ruth?" Carrie sat back down on the floor near Henry and handed him the train Ruth had been playing with earlier. He grinned and took it from her, running it over the wooden floor, making a sound like a motorcoach.

Ruth muttered under her breath about how that wasn't right before she answered. "Well, she was on the big boat with me, the one that sank," she explained as if it wasn't anything at all that she almost drowned aboard *Titanic*. "Thanks to Uncle Charlie, we both survived. Now, I keep her with me all the time."

"I see." Carrie now remembered hearing stories about how Ruth had slipped away and gone looking for her doll. She hadn't put two-and-two together to realize this was that doll—until now. "That must've been very scary. For both of you."

"It was," Ruth said with a nod. "But we had two hours to get off our boat. You'll only have eighteen minutes."

Carrie's eyebrows furrowed as she tried to understand what the child was saying to her, but just then, Ms. Meg, Ms. Kelly, and Mrs. Pendleton came into the room, followed closely by Jonathan Lane, Mr. Ashton's liegeman who was a favorite of Ruth's in particular. She darted out of the chair to rush over and hug him. Jonathan scooped her up and tossed her into the air as she giggled.

"Don't you dare drop my daughter on her crown, now, Mr. Jonathan," Kelly said in her thick Irish accent as she crept toward Lizzie. "That one is the brains of the family. You knock the sense out of her, we're all in trouble."

Jonathan stopped tossing Ruth and set her down. "I wouldn't dream of it," he assured the mother who was clearly only teasing.

Carrie smiled at the lot of them as they settled in the room, but it seemed clear there was something amiss. Ms. Meg sat on the edge of her seat rubbing her baby bump, a letter in her other hand. Her brows were furrowed as she looked at her son playing at her feet, almost as if she were seeing him, but none of it was registering.

"Is everything all right, Ms. Meg?" Carrie asked, handing Lizzie a toy she'd dropped.

It took Meg a moment to answer. She blinked a few times and then said, "What's that? Oh, yes. Everything is fine, Carrie," with the same easy smile she often wore on her face, though it was strained more than usual.

"Hardly." Kelly shook her head, sitting on the rug by the children and Carrie. "Of all the times for your mother to raise her ugly, selfish head."

Immediately, Carrie's interest perked as her eyebrows shot up. It had been ages since anyone had mentioned Mrs. Mildred Westmoreland in the Ashton home. For Kelly to do so now, Carrie knew something drastic must have transpired. "What is it?" she asked.

Ms. Meg drew in a deep breath through her nose and slowly let it out. "She's dying." She shrugged, flipping the letter around a bit before lying it down on a table next to her.

"The nerve of some people," Jonathan joked, clearly trying to lighten the mood.

Ms. Meg narrowed her eyes at him but then continued. "She's dying, and she wants me to come to Southampton to retrieve a package."

Carrie let that set in. When Ms. Meg had traveled back to

Southampton last, not too long after the *Titanic* disaster, Carrie had accompanied her. It had been her first, and only, trip across the sea—not counting the return trip, of course. She'd enjoyed her time aboard the *Mauritania*, but she wished her mistress had been more keen on getting out to explore the ship. She understood why Meg preferred to stay inside, but it hadn't been quite the adventure she wished to have enjoyed.

The idea of going back across now intrigued her. For a moment, she imagined herself sailing across the wide blue ocean, the sun setting off in the distance, the promise of a star-filled sky above her on the horizon.

But, it was evident that Ms. Meg wouldn't be going anywhere in her current state. It wouldn't be safe to sail across the ocean in her condition. Carrie let the disappointment wash over her slowly, trying to contain her expression.

"I would go for you," Kelly began, "but Daniel would have my head. And these two little ones don't need another voyage like the last one."

"It won't be like the last one," Ruth chimed in, though no one was paying her much mind. She picked up the train from earlier and made an exploding sound. Carrie stared at her a moment, but when Ms. Meg began to speak again, her attention was averted.

"I would never ask you to do that," Ms. Meg said to Kelly. "You either, Jonathan."

"I don't mind so much," the liegeman said. He perched on the edge of a desk across the room. "It's only, I might not be able to make my way back across the pond."

"What do you mean?" Ms. Pendleton asked with an amused expression. With Jonathan, one could always assume a witty joke was coming.

"I'd likely kill the old bat and get locked up in a British gaol," he said with a chuckle.

The women laughed as well, but Carrie could understand why he'd say such a thing. Mildred Westmoreland had been a horrible person. She'd abused Ms. Meg and allowed her brother-in-law to do even worse. While Carrie hadn't been privy to every bit of discussion from their last trip, she'd fallen under the impression that perhaps Mrs. Westmoreland had actually been responsible for Ms. Meg's father's death. Who would murder their own husband?

"Ms. Carrie likes boats." This time, Ruth's soft voice cut through the silence of the room.

The other adults in the room turned to look at her.

Carrie cleared her throat and straightened her gown. "Well, that is true," she said. "I wouldn't mind at all going across the ocean to get the box from your mother, Ms. Meg. That is, if you'd trust me to do such a thing. I assume that the box must be quite important that this is even under discussion."

"It is," Ms. Meg confirmed. "In her letter, my mother says that it contains some of my father's prized possessions, items I assumed she'd destroyed or sold long ago."

Carrie nodded. "Well, then, I'd be willing to go." Once again, images of herself on the boat came to mind, but this time she wasn't alone—a tall, handsome man stood next to her. Carrie felt her cheeks flame, just thinking about such a possibility. It was silly, but a woman could dream.

"It's a bit dangerous right now." Jonathan's tone was much more serious this time. "Germans have been seen in the waters between here and there."

"Germans?" Carrie's stomach knotted slightly as she considered what he was saying.

He nodded, adjusting his lean slightly. "In submersibles."

Carrie had some idea what that meant. Germans in boats under the water that were difficult to detect—carrying bombs, no doubt. She cleared her throat. "Well, that does sound a bit dangerous, but then, people get run over by motor coaches here in the city all the time, don't they?"

Ms. Meg and Ms. Kelly exchanged a puzzled look before Ms. Meg said, "Yes, I suppose so."

"So, it's possible for anyone to get hurt or killed at any time, isn't it?" Carrie concluded.

Meg held a thoughtful look for a moment before she said, "While that is true, I wouldn't want you to put yourself at risk for me, Carrie."

"I don't feel that it's a risk," Carrie concluded quickly. The urge to travel, to have a bit of an adventure, called to her. "I will happily go for you."

"You can't go on your own," Jonathan reminded her. "It wouldn't be safe for a lady to travel alone."

"I'm no lady," Carrie reminded him with a snicker.

"You are a lady," Jonathan disagreed, "and you cannot go alone."

Feeling as if the possibility of adventure was being torn away from her again, Carrie thought up a protest, but before she could speak the words aloud, Jonathan added, "I'll go with you."

2

May 1, 1915

A COOL BREEZE blew in off the ocean as Charlie Ashton found a place to park his motorcoach near where the *Lusitania* would be disembarking in just a couple of hours. Carrie took a deep breath as she opened the door, letting the salt air cleanse her lungs. Most of New York City was congested and smelled of smoke from the autos and dung from the horses that were still in service, but here, the air was crisp. It smelled like adventure.

"I'll get your bag, Carrie," Charlie said. "I'll carry it aboard for you."

"Oh, Mr. Ashton, there's no need for you to do that," she said, following him around the car. "I can manage."

"I know you can, but I want to inspect your quarters and make sure everything is in order before I leave you," he explained. He took the bag out of the car and waited for Jonathan, who was speaking in hushed tones to his significant other, Edward, to grab his luggage as well.

"I'm sure Jonathan and I can fend for ourselves." As much as Carrie appreciated working for such an attentive boss, she did worry about Mr. Ashton climbing aboard the passenger liner. She knew he wasn't fond of them.

"Nonsense." Charlie gave her a tight smile and began to walk toward the docks. It was easy to see *Lusitania*. While there were several vessels in the port, it was by far the grandest of them all.

Carrie paused to take it in, noting how the sunlight glistened off the bow. Her heartbeat quickened as she walked light on her feet behind her employer, so thankful to have this opportunity.

Behind her, she heard Jonathan and Edward talking. To anyone who didn't know better, they'd sound like good friends talking about how they would miss one another for the time that they'd be separated. Of course, Carrie knew otherwise. While she didn't envy them the judgment they would most certainly receive if anyone ever became the wiser to their arrangement, she definitely wished she had someone like that—someone to miss her when she was gone. Ms. Meg, little Henry, and the rest of the staff would miss her, but not in the same way Edward and Jonathan would miss one another.

A sea of passengers and their guests crowded around the deck. Many of them appeared to be other-than First Class passengers waiting their turn to load the boat. Charles Ashton waited for no one, and when the crew members took note of his presence, they immediately hopped into service.

"Mr. Ashton!" a man dressed in a uniform of the Cunard Line said in a friendly tone as Charlie led them past the others to the First Class Passenger entrance. "We didn't know you'd be sailing with us, sir."

"I won't be," Charlie replied, clapping the fellow on the arm like they were old friends. "A couple of my closest friends will be, and I'm here to see them off." Charlie drew the tickets he'd purchased only the day before from his pocket and showed them to the fellow.

He didn't even glance at them. "Yes, sir. Please head straight in. One of my associates will direct you toward your accommodations."

Carrie smiled at the older gentleman and thanked him. She'd always wondered what it would be like to be rich like Mr. Ashton. Perhaps while she was on the ship, a First Class Passenger, not in service to anyone for a few days, she'd find out. The bag Charlie carried was stuffed full of gowns, jewelry, and other luxury items she wouldn't typically have the opportunity to wear. But Ms. Meg had insisted she must look nice and enjoy herself, so they'd made a hasty shopping trip, and now, here she was—a lady boarding the vessel that would carry her across the ocean in style.

Another worker with just as jovial of an attitude led them to their accommodations. "Here we are!" He made a grand deal of opening the door. "One of your suites, sir. The other is here." He gestured to the next door. "There is an interior door that joins them which can be locked." He gave Carrie a nod, as if to say she wouldn't have to worry about Jonathan slipping into her bedroom at night, and Carrie almost laughed.

"Thank you kindly." Charlie slipped the man a few bills and then went inside, Carrie right behind him. Jonathan and Edward went to the next door, but once Carrie was inside her room, she could no longer pay anyone else any mind.

The sitting room was exquisite, with dark wooden furniture so polished it shone. The floral printed cushions looked inviting, and the view out the large window, just beyond her own private deck, was mesmerizing. Here, the ocean was a blue-gray with glints of sunlight sparkling off the small whitecaps, but she could only imagine the color would become more vibrant as they made it out to sea.

Charlie stepped into the adjoining room. Carrie could hardly pull her eyes away from the scene out the window but managed. In the bedroom, she had a large four-poster bed in the same wood finish as the furniture in the living room. The room wasn't as large as she remembered Ms. Meg's bedroom being on the *Mauritania*, but it would certainly do. Her room at the Ashton mansion was lovely, but somehow, this space seemed more luxurious. Perhaps because, at least for now, it was her own.

"What do you think?" Mr. Ashton asked, putting her bag away for her. "Is it satisfactory?"

"It's wonderful, Mr. Ashton. Thank you so much." She wanted to hug him but kept her hands folded in front of her instead.

"Of course. We are so grateful that you and Jonathan are willing to make this journey on Meg's behalf, we want to make sure you are more than comfortable." His grateful smile confirmed how much he meant every word.

"I'm honored that Ms. Meg has entrusted me with such a responsibility." While the idea of facing Ms. Meg's mother at the end of the journey wasn't all that appealing, Carrie couldn't think about that at the moment. She was too caught up in the notion that she was about to set sail on an enchanting voyage that held all the promise of adventure she'd been seeking. Adventure—and romance.

"You have the money I gave you?" Charlie asked.

Carrie nodded, patting the handbag she had slung over her shoulder. "I do."

"Good. Be sure to lock most of it in the safe. You don't want to be carrying it all on you. But you'll need some for tipping and the like."

"Yes, of course." While she'd never been the one responsible for such activities before, she'd observed Mr. Ashton and Ms. Meg in action hundreds of times and knew when to tip and how generous to be. "It was very kind of you to pay for everything."

"You're only here because my wife requires it," he reminded her. "That makes it my responsibility, and my pleasure." He smiled and patted her arm.

The door behind them in the sitting area opened, and Jonathan and Edward came through. "You'd better keep this locked," Edward joked. "You don't want this one coming into your bedchambers in the middle of the night." He gave Jonathan a playful jab.

Laughing, Carrie said, "For some reason, I'm not the least bit concerned."

"What do you think of your rooms?" Charlie asked Jonathan.

"Well, they're not quite as grand as *Titanic*," the liegeman began, shoving his hands in his pockets and rocking slightly, "but then, these rooms are on top of the ocean, so I prefer them."

For now.

The thought caught Carrie off-guard. Where had that come from? Perhaps it was the silly comments Ruth had made that had her thinking such morbid thoughts. She shook her head slightly, trying to clear her mind of such ugliness. Of course, they would be fine and make it safely to Liverpool to catch a train to Southampton. Then, they'd do it all in reverse. Easy as pie.

"I suppose Edward and I should get off the boat before it sets sail." Charlie's tone seemed easy-going, but Carrie didn't miss the way he turned to look out the window at the ocean, a stormy look in his eyes. He'd almost died when *Titanic* sank. Did those memories still haunt him? She didn't know how they couldn't.

And yet, Jonathan, who'd also survived the sinking, would be setting sail with her. It seemed odd how the same experience could affect two people in different ways. But then, Charlie had practically died in the cold Atlantic water, and Jonathan had been aboard a lifeboat, thanks to Meg.

Cold Atlantic water.

"Carrie?" Mr. Ashton said her name in a manner that made her suppose it wasn't the first time he'd spoken. "Are you all right?"

"Fine." She forced a smile. She really needed to get those silly thoughts out of her head and enjoy this trip. After all, she'd done this before aboard the *Mauretania* , and she'd been fine. There hadn't been the threat of U-boats in the water then, but she had to trust that they'd be safe. Otherwise, why would anyone set sail at a time like this?

"I'll walk you up," Jonathan told Edward.

"I think I'll stay here, if you don't mind," Carrie added as the gentlemen moved toward the door.

"Of course. But don't miss the disembarking. It's the best part," Charlie told her. He leaned over to give her a quick hug. "Take care, Carrie."

She hugged him back, waved at Edward, and watched the three of them disappear.

With a deep breath, Carrie turned around slowly, taking in her room. It was a lovely place, and for the next few days, it was hers—and hers alone.

Exhaling, she sank down on the couch and stared out at the sea. The furniture was just as comfortable as it looked, and as she gazed around her accommodations, she was certain she could get used to this.

Once she'd let it sink in that she was a First Class passenger, that she would be the lady of the manor for almost a week, she pulled herself up off the couch with a satisfied smile and set about making herself at home, putting her items in drawers and hanging her gowns. She was finished and perched on the edge of her bed when Jonathan knocked on the door that separated their quarters.

"We're about to set sail," he announced with a warm smile. "Do you want to come up to the promenade and wave goodbye to everyone?"

"Are Mr. Ashton and Edward still here?" she asked, standing and walking toward him.

"No, they left, but that doesn't mean we can't pretend we know someone in the crowd." He grinned at her, and Carrie laughed.

"That sounds like a fabulous idea."

Jonathan offered his arm, and the two of them went up to the First Class promenade where a crowd of finely dressed people pressed against the railings, hands raised as they said goodbye to friends and family or perfect strangers.

A giggle of glee escaped Carrie's lips as she waved at the people on shore. "Goodbye!" she shouted. "We'll see you in a few weeks!"

The passenger liner began to move beneath her as the ocean currents laid claim to *Lusitania*, taking her out to see. As New York Harbor grew smaller and smaller, Carrie's excitement bubbled over.

This was going to be the adventure of a lifetime.

3

The sensation of being out on the open water was thrilling. Carrie could stand on the balcony in her first class accommodations and stare out at the water all day. Unfortunately, she heard the sound of bugles blowing announcing it was almost time for dinner and had to pull herself away.

Jonathan knocked on the door that separated their two rooms. "Yes?" she called, turning and walking back into the living room.

"Are you about ready, my lady?" he asked with a cordial smile.

"I am," she said, her arms spread slightly to show her new gown. "Do you think I can pass as a lady? Or will I stick out like a sore thumb?"

"Well," Jonathan began, scratching his chin, "you're not exactly my type." That made her giggle. "But I think you look pretty… amazing."

"Thank you." Carrie felt her face heat, even though Jonathan's admiration was strictly of the friendly variety. She did like the blue dress Ms. Meg had helped her pick out. With jeweled fringe, the gown hung down to the new strappy blue shoes she'd also purchased. With earrings she'd borrowed from Meg, in a silver that complimented the dark blue, she felt like she could truly pass for a lady, not someone's servant.

"Shall we?" Jonathan stepped forward and offered his arm.

"Yes, let's." Carrie wrapped her arm through Jonathan's, and the two of them headed out of her room. He looked debonair in a suit that could've just as easily come from Charlie's closet. Though it was strange to see Jonathan without his signature bowler hat. Carrie assumed he wasn't wearing it that evening because he thought it was inappropriate for dinner. His dark hair looked nice slicked back. "You know," she began, keeping her voice low, "you could pass for a gentleman."

Snickering, Jonathan replied, "Don't let Edward hear you say such things. He'll expect far too much of me."

Again, Carrie found herself giggling gleefully. But she had to wonder–would Jonathan ever step out on his own? He'd most certainly obtained a bit of wealth over the years working for such a generous employer. She decided now wasn't the time to ask since they were approaching the grand dining room.

Carrie sucked in a deep breath, trying to calm her nerves. She had seen the First Class dining room on the *Mauretania*, but she hadn't walked into it as her own person, unattached to anyone else. Now, she'd have to stand on her own two feet. Thank goodness Jonathan was there with her. He certainly knew how to convince everyone that he belonged there.

"Mr. Lane, Ms. Boxhall," the well-dressed man at the door greeted them. "Right this way."

Carrie turned and lifted her eyebrows to Jonathan, wondering how in the world he knew who they were, but when Jonathan flashed her that dazzling smile of his, she understood. He must've made sure they had satisfactory dinner accommodations while she'd been standing on the balcony staring out at the sea.

Jonathan pulled Carrie's chair out for her, and she thanked him before sitting. He sat on her left, leaving a few empty chairs on her right for guests who hadn't arrived yet. As they waited for dinner to begin, Carrie looked around the room. She didn't see anyone she recognized, but the stunning outfits, the jewels and furs, and the demeanor with which everyone handled themselves assured her she was in the midst of high society.

Jonathan leaned over and whispered into her ear, "That gentleman there is Lindon Bates, the politician," he whispered. "And over there, that woman in the red dress is Frances Stephens, the socialite."

"Oh, my," Carrie said, trying not to stare as Mrs. Stephens turned in their direction. Jonathan continued to point out several ladies and gentlemen of note until the people at their table introduced themselves.

The gentleman across from her offered his hand. "Frederick Pearson."

"Delighted to meet you." She shook his hand, noting the firm grip of a businessman, though she had no idea who he was. "Carrie Boxhall."

"The pleasure is all mine. This is my wife, Mabel."

The woman nodded with a smile but didn't extend her hand. Carrie returned the smile, but then her eyes were drawn away to the two empty seats beside them as two people walked toward them. The attractive couple was clearly not a couple at all, though it seemed they knew one another. The woman, who appeared to be a couple of years younger than Carrie, was strikingly beautiful, and Carrie thought she recognized her from somewhere.

The gentleman wore one of the finest suits she'd ever seen. His dark eyes met her gaze, and a wry smile pulled up the corners of his mouth. Again, there was something familiar about him, but she wasn't quite sure what it was that made her feel that way.

"Well, look here, Emily," the newest arrival said to his companion as they reached their seats, "you're not the only gorgeous woman at our table tonight."

As if on cue, Mabel Pearson said, "Why, thank you, Victor."

His eyes widened slightly, and everyone shared a chuckle. "Naturally, I meant you as well, Mrs. Pearson," he said, his cheeks turning a bit pink. He pulled the seat out for the woman who would be sitting beside him, Emily, and the two of them joined their little group.

"I'm just teasing you, Victor." Mrs. Pearson's tone was a bit flirtatious, and Carrie could hardly blame her. The man was awfully attractive. "I'm certain you meant Ms. Boxhall."

"Ms. Boxhall?" Once again, those dark eyes were on her. "Oh, yes. I most certainly did. It's a delight to meet you." He offered his hand, but it was clear from the way he was holding it out that he didn't mean to shake hers. Rather, he intended to place a kiss on the back of her fingers.

Carrie's breath caught in her throat as she obliged. His lips, warm and soft, lingered a bit too long, making her uncomfortable for reasons she couldn't quite understand. This attractive, obviously wealthy, man was paying more attention to her than any man had in a number of years, and yet, she heard alarm bells going off in the back of her head the same way she would if there was a structure fire downtown in New York City.

"Oh, Victor, stop." Emily swatted at him until he released Carrie's hand, but Victor's eyebrows danced with mirth. "You're being ridiculous."

"What? She's a gorgeous woman, and you've already turned down my every advance, Miss Harris."

"I may be Miss Harris to the masses, but you and I both know I'm Mrs. Stein now, Victor, and I'd prefer it if you kept that in mind." She gave him another look that could only be described as annoyed before turning to Carrie. "It's lovely to meet you, Ms. Boxhall."

"Carrie, please," she found herself correcting. With their exchange, she'd finally realized who she was looking at. "I just loved your last picture show. You were absolutely mesmerizing in it."

Emily's cheeks pinked. "Oh, thank you, dear. That's very kind of you to say."

"It's true." Carrie found herself suddenly in a situation where she might lose her composure over the woman sitting across from her. She took a deep breath and tried to rein it in, but it was difficult. She'd been around plenty of socialites, but Emily Harris was a movie star.

"What about me?"

The man to her right, the one who'd escorted Emily in, Victor something-or-other, suddenly needed her attention. "Pardon?"

"Oh, come on, sweetheart. Don't pretend you didn't recognize me."

Carrie turned to look at Victor with discernment. She had to admit he did look familiar, though she couldn't remember seeing him in any picture shows. She shook her head slightly, her mouth hanging open.

Just then, the wait staff came over to their table, pouring wine and offering selections. It was distraction enough that Jonathan was able to whisper in her ear. "Victor Anderson, Carrie. The millionaire."

Carrie gaped at him, almost as shocked now as she had been before when she couldn't place the man. "Are you serious?"

Jonathan nodded. "Certain."

Carrie swallowed down the lump that had begun to form in her throat. Victor Anderson came from one of the wealthiest families in all of New York—all of America, for that matter. His reputation as a playboy preceded him. She'd seen him at plenty of gatherings but hadn't had the chance to look at him this closely. Most of the time, she'd been relegated to some other room amongst the servants pretty quickly after that.

Her thoughts immediately went to her last encounter with Mr. Anderson, rather, with his liegeman, and her stomach twisted into a tight knot. That had been several years ago. Surely, he wasn't here….

"Is something the matter, Carrie?" Victor asked, that smirk on his face that showed he knew he was the richest man on the ship. "You look unwell."

"I'm fine, Mr. Anderson," she said with as much confidence as she could muster. "Delighted to be in your company."

"So you do recognize me?" Somehow, his tone increased in arrogance, something she wouldn't have thought possible. "What is a lovely little thing like you doing on a big boat like this?"

Next to her, she felt Jonathan's leg muscles tighten, despite the fact that there were a few inches between them. She could simply sense his discomfort, most likely because she felt the same way.

"I'm going to Liverpool, of course," she said smartly. That got a chuckle out of everyone else at the table.

It did not deter Victor one bit. Leaning in so close that she could feel his warm breath on her cheek, he asked, "Business... or pleasure?"

The innuendo wrapped around that last word left Carrie with a sinking feeling as if the boat beneath her had suddenly plummeted to the bottom of the Atlantic. She had seen that look in men's eyes before, that one that told her he was on the prowl, and Victor Anderson had set his eyes on her as his next prey.

"Business," she managed to get out.

The scent of mint tangled with cigar smoke on his exhale had her leaning away. "There's always room for a bit of pleasure, isn't there, darling?"

Carrie stared, dumbfounded. She'd never had a man of his stature be quite so forward with her, and she wasn't sure what to say.

Thankfully, Jonathan didn't hesitate. "I do believe Ms. Boxhall will be too busy with her work to spend much time with anyone on this trip, Mr. Anderson."

Victor's gaze continued to linger on her face until Carrie pulled her eyes away. Then, he cleared his throat and turned to Jonathan. "Mr. Lane, isn't it?" he asked. Jonathan nodded. "Aren't you Charlie Ashton's man?" Before Jonathan could reply, Victor looked around the large, opulent dining room. "I don't see Ashton anywhere."

"Mr. Ashton is at home. His wife is about to give birth. I am also his business partner," Jonathan said in a tone that made Carrie believe it as well. Was he?

Victor nodded, not questioning Jonathan's stature at the moment, though the implication was there. Why was he in the First Class dining hall when he was nothing more than a servant? A commoner?

But then, if Anderson knew the truth about her, wouldn't he say the same thing?

Or would he assume that she was easy, the kind of girl he could manipulate because she was in want of... everything?

It was Emily who broke the awkward silence. "Mr. Pearson, you must tell us of your innovations in electrical streetcar designs. Such findings fascinate me."

"I'd be happy to tell you what I'm working on," Mr. Pearson said with a soft smile. He began to discuss the changes he was making as a consultant on several projects across the continent.

Carrie listened in, tried to enjoy her meal, and did her best to ignore the near constant stare of Victor Anderson. As a millionaire, Mr. Anderson was used to getting what he wanted.

He was about to be sorely disappointed.

4

Sunlight glinted off the surface of the water as Carrie leaned over the railing on the First Class promenade. A few moments earlier, she'd heard some children giggling and pointing out in the distance. She thought she'd heard one of the little girls say something about there being dolphins in the water. Try as she may, Carrie didn't see any, and since the group had since moved on, she reckoned there likely wasn't anything to see.

But then, the majestic oceanscape before her was beautiful enough. While it would've been nice to see a bottlenose or two popping out of the water, she couldn't complain. The water was so blue out here, so enchanting, she could easily spend hours staring out at it. In fact, she had. Since she'd come aboard the day before, she'd spent an endless amount of time just watching the waves roll off the side of the passenger liner.

Jonathan had been with her a few moments earlier but had seen an acquaintance and went off to have a closer inspection of the lifeboats. He'd invited Carrie to come along, but she had decided to stay behind and stare out at the water. While it made perfect sense to her that Jonathan would want to know everything there was to learn about the lifeboats, considering what had happened to him on Titanic,

Carrie refused to be concerned about it. To her, this was the adventure of a lifetime, and she couldn't imagine anything terrible happening to her or anyone else on this ship. They would arrive in Liverpool as expected, and she'd be on her merry way to Southampton.

The worst thing about this trip would be facing that old hag, Mildred Westmoreland.

"You simply must join me this evening," a familiar male voice said from just around the corner. Carrie found herself freezing in place, not sure what to do. Was it too late to duck under cover somehow?

"Oh, now, I already told you, I'm busy," a woman's voice replied. She giggled, but it was clear to Carrie that the man inviting her to join him was not as desirable as he seemed to think, and if the voice matched the image in her head, she knew why.

For some reason, she was still standing in the same place, despite every alarm in her mind telling her to get out of there. Just as she turned her head, the couple came around the corner, and once again, she found herself face-to-face with Victor Anderson.

Carrie swallowed hard, wishing she'd listened to that voice in her head that had told her to run, but now, his eyes were on hers, and that smile that reminded her a bit of a wolf narrowing its gaze at its prey fell into place on his handsome face.

"Very well then, Lola–"

"It's Lily," the woman said sharply, suddenly more interested in him now that he wasn't so amused by her.

"Right. Lily. I'll see you later." Victor let go of Lily's arm and tipped his hat to Carrie. "Well, Ms. Boxhall. Fancy meeting you here." He turned the charm up several numbers on the dial and strolled toward her.

Sighing, Carrie reminded herself to be polite. Even though this gentleman had a reputation for being quite the womanizer, he was still a wealthy socialite, and her employers would appreciate it if she could get along with him, she assumed. Not that Ms. Meg or Mr. Ashton would ever expect her to put up with any nonsense from any man.

"Good afternoon, Mr. Anderson." She managed a smile but didn't turn away from where she'd been looking out over the railing.

"Come now, Carrie. Don't you think we should be on a first-name basis after the dinner we shared last night?" His tone was teasing as he sidled up next to her, standing far too close for her liking. The spicy smell of his cologne made even the pleasant salt air fragrance from the ocean seem unsavory, and Carrie found herself turning her head away from him just to inhale.

"I'm not certain we know each other that well," she said, clearing her throat. "For example, I'm not sure that you understand that, while I am a First Class passenger upon this ship, in reality, I'm nothing more than a lady in waiting." While she hated to speak ill of herself, as she'd worked hard to gain her position with Ms. Meg, Carrie hoped to remind Mr. Anderson that he was of a different social class than her in life outside of *Lusitania*. At the very least, perhaps she could feel out his motivations.

His sly grin widened, showing his pearly white teeth. "Yes, of course I've deduced that. But here, you and I are equals, aren't we, Carrie? Wouldn't you like to take this fantasy of yours of being a socialite one step further and spend some time with the wealthiest man on the ship?" His confident smile told her he assumed she was just playing hard to get and would cave soon enough at the notion of sharing his company–and his bed.

Carrie took a deep breath and turned away from him again. She wasn't that kind of woman. She'd had romantic relationships in the past, the kind that never really led to anything, but she had loved those gentlemen, each in their own way, and had learned something about herself in each of those relationships. Likewise, she'd found what it was she was truly looking for in a man, and at her age, she was ready to find the right one and begin to think about her future.

The last thing she wanted or needed was to be the toy of a wealthy man to be discarded the moment they landed in Liverpool.

"Mr. Anderson," she began, but she didn't get very far before someone else spoke his name as well, another gentleman, and when

Carrie turned to see who it was addressing the millionaire, her breath caught in her lungs.

"Mr. Anderson?" A smooth, deep voice Carrie recognized but hadn't heard in a number of years sang to her ear as she turned her head to look at a familiar face.

Handsome, with strong features, dark hair, and warm brown eyes, the man came to a stop right in front of her, but his attention was on Victor, not her. In fact, he hadn't seemed to notice her at all. In Carrie's mind, that was a good thing; it would give her a moment to compose herself.

"What is it, Robert?" Victor asked, huffing in annoyance. "Can't you see that I'm busy?"

"That telegraph you were expecting from Mr. Peterson came through," Robert continued, holding out a piece of paper. "You said you wanted it right away." It was then that he turned his attention to Carrie. "Beg your pardon, miss–Miss… Boxhall?"

Carrie felt her cheeks heat as Robert's chocolate eyes melted over her. "Hello, Robert," she said, trying to sound nonchalant but feeling as if she was failing miserably. "It's lovely to see you."

"You as well." His smile reached his eyes as he took her in. "It's been so long. I don't think I've seen you since the wedding."

"That's right," Carrie started, but before she could finish her sentence, Victor interrupted.

"If you don't mind, Robert, I think you have duties to attend to elsewhere, don't you?" Victor moved a few steps closer to her, resting his hand on her arm.

Instinctively, Carrie pulled away. "Really, Mr. Anderson, as I was trying to tell you before, I don't really feel that you and I have much in common."

"And I believe I told you to call me Victor." His smile widened, once again showing his teeth. His canines seemed particularly sharp today.

Carrie cleared her throat. "I believe it's time for me to meet Mr. Lane. We made an appointment to meet up earlier." She took a step away from

Victor, brushing against Robert as she did so. Tiny pinpricks of electricity shot up her arm. She wished she had time to linger, to discuss the last time they'd seen one another. Robert was right–it had been at Ms. Meg and Mr. Ashton's wedding. He had been in the service of one of Mr. Ashton's other associates at the time, but he'd spoken of going to work for Mr. Anderson. So when she'd established who Victor was at dinner the night before, she could only hope that Robert was here.

Now, here he was, standing before her, a concerned look on his face, and she was in the process of trying to move away from him, even though it was the last thing on earth she wanted to do. How many times had she dreamt of him since that night? At the wedding, he'd asked her to dance, and he'd swept her away in his arms. They'd laughed and whispered to one another about what they would do one day if they were carefree and able to follow their ambitions, rather than being tied down to their employers. Perhaps it was the wine speaking, but Carrie had told him then that she wanted to run away with him.

It had all been wishful thinking, though, and time had marched on without either of them even speaking to one another. She had considered trying to track him down a time or two but was never brave enough to do so.

"Carrie," Victor's arm on her shoulder interrupted her thoughts. He pulled her back a little more forcefully than he should have, and her footing failed her. The shoes she was wearing were just as foreign to her as the new gown. Carrie felt herself slipping on the slick promenade decking.

Another arm reached out to grab her. Robert's quick reflexes prevented her from falling as he hooked her around the waist. "Careful there, Miss Boxhall." His tone was gentle, reassuring. But when he lifted his eyes to his employer, his expression changed. "I'd be more than happy to escort Miss Boxhall to her appointment, sir, so that you can respond to your telegraph."

Victor cleared his throat, the pressure from his hand on her shoulder not changing as he said, "That won't be necessary. Carrie and I are good friends. Better friends than the two of you–I'm certain."

It was a warning. One Carrie heard loud and clear. Victor wanted Robert to leave them be.

Yet, his warm brown eyes landed soundly on her face again. His eyebrows raised inquisitively. Did Carrie truly want him to leave her alone with Victor?

Of course, she didn't. But she also didn't want Robert to get in trouble. She looked around and saw several couples and families milling about. Victor couldn't hurt her here. "It's fine," she assured Robert, missing the warmth of his hand as he withdrew it from her. "Thank you, Robert."

He continued to hold her gaze for a moment before nodding and returning his attention to Victor. "I'll be in the room then, sir."

"Yes, yes," Victor said dismissively. "I know you have much work to do."

Robert gave her another look to make sure she was all right and then turned and walked away. Carrie couldn't help but follow him with her eyes until he'd disappeared into the crowd.

As soon as he was gone, Victor resituated himself so that he was standing in front of Carrie, his hand still on her shoulder, and her back to the railing. "Now, Miss Carrie... where were we?" Victor's smile was sly. Some women might've found him cunning, but Carrie felt her stomach flip over.

She took a deep breath, not sure what to say. "We were—"

"Just about to meet some friends. Pardon me, Mr. Anderson, but we can't be late." Jonathan swooped in out of nowhere, brushing past Mr. Anderson and taking her by the arm. Carrie's feet were moving before she could even process what had happened. She heard Victor muttering to himself behind her, but Jonathan didn't slow down–and neither of them looked back.

5

Robert tried not to rush back to his room. He knew he was letting his emotion carry him away, and he didn't want to be rude to the other passengers he passed in the narrow halls as he found his way back to his room–Victor's room, that was.

A prominent couple Robert recognized from all the parties he'd attended over the years in service to others came out of their room and almost ran into him. Robert skirted out of the way, plastering himself against the wall as the so-called gentleman turned and gave him a nasty glare.

"Pardon me, sir," Robert said, tipping his head. The older man only made a "hmph" noise in the back of his throat and led his wife on down the hall. Taking a deep breath, Robert did his best to let it go. It was clear by his suit–his uniform, in actuality–that he was only in the First Class portion of the ship because he was a servant.

Perhaps that was all he would ever be.

No, he couldn't think like that. One day, he'd be a First Class passenger here because he was wealthy and important, just like Victor Anderson and the others. As he came to the correct room, he slipped inside, trying to convince himself that his dream could come true.

Robert went about the tasks Victor had assigned him earlier that morning, including ironing his suit for dinner that evening, and as he did so, he let his mind wander. He'd saved up plenty of money over the course of the years. His last employer, Matthew, had been a terrible drunk when Robert had first met him, but he'd turned it around once he'd gotten married. The man had paid well, though. It was a pity that they'd parted ways. Once he wed, Matthew became a changed man, one who was more than bearable to be around. But his wife had recently inherited several staff members from her late parents, and one of them was a liegeman who'd served her family well over the years. She actually thought of him as a grandfather. Therefore, Robert was replaced.

He'd found a job with Victor pretty quickly, which he'd been grateful for at the time. Running the hot iron over Victor's already wrinkle-free white dress shirt, he thought about how silly he'd been. Not that Victor didn't pay well, but the arrogant playboy was difficult to put up with. Unlike his last employer, who had been more like a friend or a mentor to him, Victor barked orders at him. He often spoke to him like he thought he was an idiot, or perhaps an uneducated child. In actuality, Robert had attended a few years of college but had to drop out before he finished his engineering degree because his mother had taken ill, and he needed to provide for her. While a good deal of his earnings still went to provide for her, he'd managed to save up some.

And it was the thought of that money that kept his mind occupied as he continued to run the hot iron over the rest of Victor's suit until it was so well pressed it wouldn't wrinkle for hours, no matter what Victor found himself doing.

Robert shook his head, hanging the suit back up and turning to his next assignment, polishing Victor's shoes. The thought of the sort of trouble that man could get himself into left him swearing under his breath. How many times had he woken Victor up for an important meeting only to find him with a woman or two in his bed? Robert had always been the one to help them find their stockings, get them presentable, and walk them out, always assuring them that Mr. Anderson would call on them soon.

Of course, the jackass never did.

Taking a deep breath, Robert continued to run the brush over Victor's shoes until he could see his face in the reflection. These were perfect for later that evening when Mr. Anderson would find himself busy entertaining the other rich folks in the First Class dining room.

Well, not all of them were rich.

Carrie.

He let himself think of her for the first time since he'd been dismissed from her presence. For a moment there, he'd thought perhaps he should stay and make sure the hand Mr. Anderson had on her was welcome, but Carrie had let him know she was fine in her own way. He pictured her beautiful face, and for just a brief time, allowed himself to slip back into how they'd interacted at the Ashtons' wedding. She'd been so joyful that night, so full of spirit. They'd made promises to one another that someday they'd enjoy another dance, and maybe, just maybe, they'd go off on their own adventures one day.

It had been a silly conversation, fueled by wine and the knowledge that the woman she worked for, someone she cared deeply for, was happy and marrying the man of her dreams.

Still, as Robert lifted his head for a moment and looked out at the deep blue water around him, he couldn't help but wonder; when Carrie Boxhall closed her eyes at night, who was the man she was dreaming about?

Scoffing, he mumbled, "Not me," and continued to polish the shoe. No, it looked as if she had done well for herself. Perhaps she had already married some wealthy gentleman, and that's what she was doing aboard *Lusitania* dressed in such a fancy gown. He swallowed hard, trying not to let it get to him. Carrie was a kind woman, a beautiful woman, and she deserved all the happiness in the world. He could never give her that kind of life.

Or could he? Setting Victor's shoe aside and picking up the other one, he thought about the invention he was working on. He'd started sketching the idea for it back when he'd worked for Matthew. Being a good man, when his employer had noticed what he was working on, he'd offered some advice. Not that Matthew was an engineer. But he knew people–lots of people–and in a matter of days, Robert found himself speaking with some of the most brilliant minds in all of New York City. They'd given him some pointers about how to improve his idea, and then they'd helped him find the right people to move forward with the project. He'd even gotten a prototype made.

Then, the situation had changed, and Robert had found himself working for Victor Anderson, one of the most arrogant men in all of New York. Anderson hadn't cared at all to listen to Robert's ideas for improving motor coach engines to make them run more efficiently on less fuel. He'd told him he was a foolish man and needed to focus on the important things in life–like getting his dress shoes ready for dinner. Since then, Robert had done very little with his invention.

In times like this, he wondered if it was a possibility he could actually make something of it. If he had the backing of someone more like Matthew, someone who was kind and generous, perhaps he could get his invention in front of the right people, and he could make his ideas a reality.

The sound of the stateroom door opening brought his attention out of his thoughts and back to the shoe–and the man who would be wearing it. Robert continued to brush while Victor slammed things around for a few minutes.

Eventually, he wheeled around to face Robert. "Why the hell do you think it's all right to come and interrupt me when I'm obviously engaged in speaking to someone?"

Robert looked up, eyebrows raised, trying to choose an answer that wouldn't make his boss even more upset. Of all the choices raising through his mind, none of them seemed benign enough for the angry millionaire. All he could manage to eke out was, "I beg your pardon, sir."

"Beg my pardon?" Victor gave a half-amused, half-irritated chuckle. "Is that all you have to say for yourself?"

Apparently, even that wasn't good enough for the man. Robert decided not to say more if he could help it. Victor got in moods like this whenever his plans with a woman went awry. All Robert could do now was hope this meant that Carrie had turned him down. If she was indeed married, there wasn't a chance in hell she'd go sauntering off with Anderson. Robert knew her well enough to understand that she was the kind of woman who would stay loyal. But then, he also thought she wasn't the sort of girl who'd be interested in Victor and his approach anyway. It was always clear his boss liked his women fast and loose. Carrie was too smart to fall for his flattering.

"Answer me!" Victor insisted, tossing a few papers from the table in Robert's direction. They fell harmlessly on the floor.

"I'm sorry, sir," Robert began, keeping his tone in check as much as he could. "I didn't mean to interrupt. I thought you would want to know about the message. I'm sure Ms. Boxhall didn't mind."

"She didn't mind one bit." Victor went over to the bar and poured himself a glass of scotch. It seemed a little early to be drinking, but who was Robert to tell him what to do? "I'm gonna see her later tonight."

Robert paused mid-swipe, wondering if that were true. Would Carrie really go out with a man like Victor? Surely not. He cleared his throat and put all of his attention on the task at hand, not willing to let his imagination get the better of him.

"Dame like that can't say no to a fellow like me. You know she still works for the Ashtons, right?" He laughed and tossed back his scotch like it was water. "She can smell the money on me, though. She wants what I've got. Too bad all she's gonna get is what's in my pants." Robert didn't turn his head to watch the man crudely grab his crotch. He'd seen Victor do that enough times before to know exactly what he was up to.

Instead, Robert pretended like the shoe in his hand still needed polishing until Victor had had enough self-indulgence. "I'm going to go lie down for a bit. All that brandy in the smoking room last night is getting to me a little. Wake me up in an hour."

"Yes, sir." Robert glanced at the clock across the room and noted the time. He would do as he was told, but he knew Victor wouldn't be ready to get up in an hour. He'd sleep for two at least.

Once his employer had retired to his bed chambers, Robert put his shoes where they belonged and tidied up, putting away the polishing kit and picking up the papers off the floor.

Carrie wasn't married–but she was seeing Victor later that night. It didn't add up for him. What other possibilities were there?

Either Victor was flat-out lying, which was a possibility, or he was exaggerating. Maybe he just meant he'd see Carrie at dinner.

Was she really going out with him? Robert would find out soon enough as Victor would bring her back to these very chambers to have his way with her. Could Robert stand in the other room while Victor used up the most interesting woman he'd ever met? He didn't think so.

Sighing, he let his eyes focus back on the water outside. He hoped that Victor wasn't telling him the truth and Carrie truly wanted to have nothing to do with the man because, if what Victor said was true, then Carrie wasn't the woman he'd always thought she was.

6

Carrie and Jonathan sat side by side in lounge chairs on the First Class Promenade. She'd hardly said a word since he'd appeared from nowhere, ready and able to save her from Victor and his amorous ways. Once again, Jonathan Lane had come to the rescue. Carrie wondered how many times in his life he'd been the one to save the day and decided to let her thoughts linger there rather than on the unscrupulous millionaire who'd been after her attention.

"What exactly did he say to you?" Jonathan asked, keeping his voice low.

On his other side sat a young lady who was probably only around twelve years of age. Carrie studied her face for a moment, thinking she looked a bit like Ruth, though this girl was blonde.

"Carrie?"

Jonathan's voice cut through her thoughts. She'd been trying to avoid going back over the conversation, but it seemed he was insisting upon it. "Oh, he basically tried to leverage my position against me. He said that someone like me would do very well to be with him, that sort of thing." That was the gist of it. Carrie didn't want to tell him word for word. It was bad enough just having some of Victor's statements bouncing around in her head.

"And no one else came over to intervene?" Jonathan made a fist with one hand and tapped it against the open palm of his other. It was evident he was irritated, if not downright upset, about the interaction. But Victor was a rich, powerful man, and even though their employer was even more so, Charlie wasn't on the boat.

"Well, someone did come to see if I was all right," Carrie admitted. Visions of Robert's face when she'd told him that she was fine flittered through her mind. He would put himself in an impossible position if he went against the man who paid him, so she'd had to make Robert think she was fine.

But then, what did that make him think of her?

"What happened?" he asked, leaning back in his seat and dropping his hands so that he was no longer punching himself.

She shook her head. "Nothing. I just told the gentleman I was fine, and he went on his way." She didn't want to mention Robert to Jonathan. They knew one another, for one thing, and she didn't want Jonathan to bring up the wedding and how she'd danced with the man as if she thought he hung the moon.

Thinking of those chocolate brown eyes, the way his hair swooped to one side, his muscular build, he probably would've been capable of hanging the moon....

"Well, I hate to say it," Jonathan chimed in, interrupting her thoughts once more–for the better, "but I think perhaps you should do all that you can to avoid Mr. Anderson for the rest of our trip."

Carrie scoffed, a strange mix between a laugh and a sigh coming out of her mouth as she stared at him. Then, she realized he was serious. "Wait–you think I should essentially lock myself in my chambers until the voyage is over? Don't be ridiculous, Jonathan."

"I'm serious, Carrie. Unless I'm with you to keep you out of harm's way, I think you should stay in your room and spend your days staring at the ocean out there. It's the same body of water as this one, you know?" He gestured at the great blue sea before them, a jesting smile on his face.

"Yes, I am aware." She shook her head. "But Jonathan, you'll recall that the last time I made this trip I slept almost the entire time. It was so boring sitting in our rooms with Ms. Meg and Mr. Ashton. I'd hated it. I can't imagine having to do that again. I'm sure that Mr. Anderson will find someone else that tickles his fancy soon enough, and when he does, he'll leave me alone. Besides, it's not as if I'll ever be alone in his company."

Jonathan began to shake his head before she even finished her statement. He pulled his hat off and slicked back his hair. "I don't know, Carrie. Men like that see women like you as a challenge."

"Women like me?" She pretended to be offended. Though she had no idea what he meant by the statement, she was sure it was nothing bad.

"That's right. Women like you with morals and scruples," he clarified. "He's used to getting exactly what he wants from whomever he wants it from, and with you, he's going to have to learn to understand a word he's never heard in his life."

'What word is that?"

"No," he replied curtly.

Carrie would've guessed that's the word he meant. She stifled a smile. "Listen, I understand you want to keep me safe, and I appreciate it. But I think I'll be just fine."

"I'll go in and speak to the kind folks in charge of dinner and see if we can have our table switched," he proposed. "I'm sure there are plenty of people who would be completely enraptured at the thought of dining with Victor Anderson."

"That is a good idea." Not having to sit by him at dinner would give her a better chance to keep herself out of his line of sight and off his mind.

"I don't blame you for not wanting to miss out on adventures." The pretty blonde girl on the other side of Jonathan's voice was light as air as the breeze lifted it to Carrie's ear.

A bit surprised to hear her speak, Carrie leaned around Jonathan to see her. "What's that, miss?" she asked with a friendly smile.

"I said I shouldn't want to miss out on the adventures we may encounter on the sea either." Her accent was British, and her manners were polite and kind.

By the looks of the older woman on the other side of her, it was clear the young woman must be wealthy. The scrunched up mouth and pouty eyes looked every bit like a proper British governess to Carrie.

"Where are you traveling to?" Jonathan asked her, his demeanor changing instantly now that he was speaking to a child. "Are you going home from a holiday abroad?"

The young woman shook her head. "No, I'm afraid not. I'm headed to boarding school for summer session," she replied with a deep sigh.

"Oh? Are you not excited about such an interesting endeavor?" Jonathan's tone conveyed to Carrie that he was trying his best to make the girl feel better about where she was headed. She obviously had no choice in the matter.

With her long blonde hair dancing around her shoulders like ribbons, catching the sunlight and shining almost like spun gold, she continued to shake her head. "I didn't want to leave home."

"You'll be fine," the gruff woman on the far side of her said without so much as turning her head.

The girl cleared her throat. "Mrs. Smythe believes I should take advantage of the opportunity afforded to me." She spoke in the tone an older woman might use to try to convey to a youngster that they needed to accept their fate.

"Mrs. Smythe is a wise woman," Jonathan concluded. He smiled at the woman, but she still refused to turn attention to her ward or anyone else. Once she made it clear she had no interest, Jonathan extended his hand to the young girl. "I'm Jonathan Lane."

She looked at his hand for a moment as if assessing whether this stranger was the kind one was allowed to speak to before slipping her much smaller hand into his palm. "Hannah Murphy."

"Pleased to meet you. This is my friend, Carrie Boxhall. We are from New York."

Carrie leaned around Jonathan to shake Hannah's hand. "Lovely to meet you, dear," she said. The girl's grasp was firmer than she'd expected. "Where are you from?"

"I'm from Liverpool originally, but my parents moved us to New York a few years ago. My father is in the steel industry–was in the steel industry." Hannah's eyes shifted so that she was looking at the decking beneath their chairs.

Carrie couldn't help but let a small, "Oh," escape her lips as she realized Hannah had lost her father. "I'm so very sorry."

"It was an automobile accident." Hannah looked up then, sucking in a breath and righting her posture as she'd no doubt been coached to do by Mrs. Smyth or someone a bit more interested in the child. "My mother passed away as well."

With that, Carrie covered her mouth with both hands as Jonathan gasped in shock. He spoke first. "That's tragic, dear Hannah. I'm so very sorry to hear of your loss. Was it recent?"

She nodded. "In February. The roads were slick. It was a terrible accident."

"I'm also very sorry." Carrie reached around Jonathan and took her hand, squeezing it. "You're so young to have lost both parents."

"Thank you." Hannah took a second to breathe, and Carrie could see in her face that she was trying not to cry. No doubt she'd been told to suck it up or something of that nature. "At any rate, I'll be continuing my studies in Liverpool now that I am an... orphan."

Carrie wanted to offer to take the child in, to take her home, to raise her as her own flesh and blood, but that wouldn't be appropriate, and it was clear that the Murphys had left their daughter some means to get by on. She was dressed well, her hair was immaculate, and she was a First Class passenger on her way across the ocean.

"Well, if there's anything either of us can do for you while you're on your journey to school, please let us know," Jonathan offered, and Carrie nodded along with him. "You seem like an intelligent, kind young woman, and we hope that you have a pleasant journey, perhaps with a bit of the adventure you spoke of, and that your studies go well once you're back in Liverpool."

"That's very kind of you." Hannah's face brightened, and Carrie imagined that was because she now saw the opportunity to escape from her governess, at least for a little while. "Actually, I've heard there may be some dolphins swimming alongside our ship from time to time."

"Would you like to go have a look?" Carrie offered, getting to her feet. "We can stand over there by the railing where Mrs. Smythe can keep an eye on you."

Mrs. Smythe didn't even acknowledge her name being spoken, not even with a grunt or a flicker of an eyelash.

"Oh, yes. Let's!" Hannah practically leapt off her seat and moved over to the railing with Carrie. Jonathan got up as well, but he stood back a bit. Carrie had the idea that he was more interested in looking for wayward billionaires than swimming mammals.

As they stared out at the water looking for any sort of movement, Carrie said quietly, "I am very sorry about your parents."

Hannah pushed up on her tiptoes, her hand raised above her eyes to help block the sun. "Thank you. I am, too, but I didn't really know them that well. I attended boarding school in New York. My father left it in his will that I should go back to Liverpool if something should happen to him so that I would be closer to his sister, my aunt."

"It's good that you have someone waiting for you there." For a moment, Carrie felt silly for thinking she should adopt the child. She did have a family, after all.

Hannah shrugged. "I don't really know any of my family. My friends back at school were more like family to me. In my experience, friends are better than family."

Carrie considered that for a moment. She had parents, a sister, and some cousins back home, but she hadn't seen any of them in a long time and only spoke to them on the phone about once a year. When she thought of who her family truly was, images of Ms. Meg, Baby Henry, Mr. Ashton, Jonathan, and Kelly's family came to mind. "I think you're right."

But then, one day, she did hope to have a family–a husband, some children. A proper family. She could picture them in her mind, too.

And when she pictured her husband, the face was familiar. Handsome, with dark eyes and dark hair.

7

The tinkle of silverware on fine china and the murmur of laughter filled Carrie's ears as she sat comfortably in her new seat in the First Class dining lounge. While her view of the ocean was partially blocked now, due to a column in the way, she preferred this seating arrangement to the one she'd endured the evening before.

Jonathan introduced the two of them to the three other couples sitting at the table. Everyone smiled politely, the couple to their left stating that they were the Gordon family from London. They seemed a bit more reserved than the other people at the table.

"Tell us about yourselves," a woman just a few years older than Carrie, by the looks of her, insisted, raising her glass of wine before she took a sip. Her short brown hair was cut fashionably, with a small curl that framed her face, and her blue gown was elegantly decorated with tiny gems that might've been real sapphires. "Are you a couple?"

Jonathan, who'd been taking a bite of his chicken, nearly choked. As he coughed, Carrie patted him on the back and answered for them. "No, no. Just good friends."

"Ooh." The woman waggled her eyebrows at them in a way that implied that she believed they were sneaking around together for some reason. Carrie probably should've been offended, but there was something about this woman that made it all seem like it was in jest.

"You'll have to excuse my wife," the man next to her said, wrapping his arm around the back of her chair as he smiled over at her. "Maude has a way of being quite cheeky when she wants to be. It's all in good fun, though."

"Oh, Lloyd, allow a woman a little bit of scandal in her life, won't you?" Maude said back, tapping him on the chest with the back of her hand.

"We share an employer," Jonathan finally managed to get out. Knowing how important it was to him to keep up the charade of being interested in women, Carrie didn't dare to say more about his particular situation. "Carrie and I are traveling together on business."

"Shame," Maude said, taking a long sip of her wine. "My version is much better."

The older gentleman sitting on the other side of Lloyd chuckled under his breath. "I'm Richard Shaw, and this is my wife Wilma." He gestured at the woman on his other side who gave Carrie a curt smile. "Where were the two of you seated last night?" His tone was congenial, full of curiosity.

"We were seated over there," Jonathan explained, gesturing in the general direction of their former table.

"And why did you ask to be moved?" Wilma wanted to know.

Carrie opened her mouth to answer, but before she could get any words out, Maude spoke up. "Were you seated by Victor Anderson?"

Unsure of how to respond, Carrie raised an eyebrow, mulling over her words.

"Because," Maude continued, "I know first-hand what a jackass he can be."

"Language, dear." Lloyd shook his head slightly and picked up his glass. Carrie assumed by his tone that he didn't really mind if she swore but felt obligated to attempt to rein her in.

"What? It's true, isn't it?" She leaned over closer to Carrie. "He can't seem to keep it in his pants to save his life."

Her eyes bulging, Carrie tried not to laugh. Maude was so

different from most of the wealthy women she was used to seeing in places such as this. How lovely was it to think one could be so direct and open?

"Whatever she's saying, pay her no mind." Lloyd gave an exasperated sigh. "The two of them have known one another for years, and they simply don't get along."

"How could we? I found him coming on to my lady's maid in the women's lounge at a young girl's birthday party one year. It was very inappropriate." Maude shook her head.

"Seems she does know what the word inappropriate means." The remark from Wilma was so quiet, Carrie almost wasn't sure she heard her correctly until Maude scoffed. It seemed Jonathan and Carrie weren't the only ones unenamored by their original table mates.

"Mr. Anderson is a unique individual," Jonathan said, trying to keep the conversation as tempered as possible. Carrie knew he would never say something bad about someone like Victor in public, not unless it was completely warranted.

"And what do you do for a living?" It was clear that Richard was trying to change the subject.

"We are in the employment of Mr. and Mrs. Charles Ashton," Jonathan explained.

"Oh, lovely family." Wilma finally approved of something.

As dinner went on, the conversation flowed freely amongst three of the couples while the fourth sat in near silence. Carrie assumed they simply didn't want to partake in the chatter, which was fine with her. Though she often felt the heavy gaze of someone seated across the room from her, she refused to turn her head to look in the direction of Victor Anderson. If he wanted to continue to obsess over her, that was his choice, but she refused to play his games.

By the time they were finished eating, she was glad she'd gotten to know Maude and hoped they'd be seated by each other for the rest of the trip. She was an amusing, intriguing woman, someone Carrie wished she could be more like. Of course, she'd never have Maude's wealth, but she thought she could get along just fine with only half her wit and charm.

"Come along, Carrie," Jonathan said as they left the table. "I'll walk you back to your room." He offered his arm like a true gentleman.

"Oh, no, Jonathan. You need to go spend some time in the lounge. Lloyd and Richard both said they were headed there. You should go continue your discussion." The gentlemen had been discussing some sort of improvement to one of the machines they all used in their factories, and while Carrie wasn't interested enough to pay too much attention, she knew it was important to Jonathan. It was information he could pass along to Mr. Ashton.

Jonathan's eyes scanned the room. Carrie could tell he was looking for Victor. She looked around, too, but Mr. Anderson was nowhere to be seen. She found herself letting go a sigh of relief. Not having to worry about the penetrating stare of the billionaire who simply wouldn't leave her alone filled her with relief.

"I'll walk you back to the room and then go to the smoking lounge," Jonathan insisted, patting her hand where it rested on his arm. "That way, I won't have to worry about you."

"You don't have to worry about me now," she insisted. "There will be plenty of people out strolling this evening, just like there were last night after dinner. Besides, Mr. Anderson is likely already in the smoking lounge. He will want to take advantage of the opportunity to force everyone else to listen to how intelligent he is."

Chuckling, Jonathan said, "While that's likely true, I'd feel better if you let me escort you."

Just then, one of Jonathan's acquaintances Carrie recognized from New York called out to him to come with them to the lounge. "There, you see? You have to go. I'll be fine." They were nearly at the prome-nade now, and she didn't want to keep him any longer. The sun had gone down over the horizon, but a golden band radiated across the surface of the ocean in the distance. It didn't even seem like night yet. Nothing at all seemed unsafe about walking back to her room alone. She could even hear chatter and laughter from other people walking along the deck.

Jonathan stared at her for a moment, arching an eyebrow, before he finally said, "Fine. I'll go. But if Victor isn't there, and he doesn't materialize quickly, I'll be following you."

"Deal." Carrie patted him on the shoulder and turned away from him, giggling as she went. Jonathan was always so protective. It was one of the things she liked most about him.

She took her time walking along next to the railing, looking out over the inky sea. Her mind began to wander to the possibilities that lie out there, beyond the horizon. What if she didn't go back to New York City? What if she hopped on another boat in Britain and headed off on a new adventure?

"Well, I guess you weren't too fond of the company at our mutual table last night?"

Victor's voice startled her. Carrie turned to find him standing in the shadows, leaning on the side of the ship, a cigarette hanging from between his lips. As he strolled over toward her, he dropped it on the deck and mashed it out.

Something about the look in his eyes was frightening to her. She spun around, looking for someone nearby who could potentially help her, but the crowd from before was gone. Either they had headed off to their rooms already or strolled right past her to a different part of the ship. The sky grew darker by the moment, and she was all alone—with Victor Anderson.

"I'm sorry, Mr. Anderson," she began, trying to step around him.

"Call me Victor." His hand clamped down on her elbow. "We're about to get to know each other quite well, Miss Carrie. No reason for formality."

Carrie attempted to yank her arm free of his grasp, but his fingers sank into her skin. Pain radiated up her arm. "Let go of me," she insisted. "You're hurting me."

A maniacal laugh seeped from between his lips. "Oh, come on. Girl like you? I bet you like it rough."

Offended and terrified, Carrie tried to get away again, wondering where Jonathan was. Surely, he'd come and check on her soon since Victor obviously wasn't in the lounge. She tried to look over his shoulder, back the way she'd come, but he moved to block her view. Had she walked too far when she was lost in her thoughts?

"Come on. Let's go back to my room, and I'll show you how a real man feels when he's deep inside of you." Victor took a few steps backward, tugging on her arm. "I know you feel like you have to keep up the facade of not wanting me, but there's no one around. You can drop the act."

"I'm not acting. Let me go!" Carrie pulled back with her arm as hard as she could and brought the heel of her shoe down on his toe. Victor groaned and let go of her momentarily, giving her enough time to take a few hurried steps away from him, but he recovered quickly, his hand darting out to snatch her by the arm again.

"You little–" Victor began, but he was quickly cut off by a deep voice resounding from the shadows.

"I believe she said no."

Carrie's breath caught in her throat as she peered into the darkness. Who was this man who'd come to rescue her? It wasn't Jonathan. He was too tall to be her friend. With her heart racing in her chest, she prayed he was there to help and not another man who thought he could take advantage of her simply because she was alone.

8

"What the hell do you think you're doing?"

Victor Anderson was beyond pissed as he squared up to the man who'd stepped out of the shadows. Carrie took a deep breath and stepped backward the moment she realized who it was that had come to her aid.

As much as she wanted Robert's help, she knew he'd be in trouble with his employer if he didn't tread lightly. He'd already intervened on her behalf once, and Mr. Ashton hadn't appreciated it. Judging by the way Victor was glaring at him now, Carrie had to assume that Robert had already overstepped.

"It's fine," she said, as she had the day before. "Thank you, Robert." Unlike last time, she didn't attempt to stay where she was near Mr. Anderson. Since Robert had already insinuated himself between them, it was easy for her to get away from Victor now. Without another word, she stepped around Robert, hoping her words were enough to calm the situation down and let them restore their relationship.

But she wasn't waiting around to find out what happened next. Instead, she rushed toward the doorway that led inside and hastily made her way to her room, not paying attention to anyone she passed, even those who asked if she was all right. She must've looked a fright, rushing as quickly as she could, her skirts pulled up away from her shoes so she didn't trip. Still, she couldn't worry about that at the moment. Her only concern was to put enough distance between herself and Victor Anderson that he could no longer threaten her.

Next time, she'd do herself a favor and listen to Jonathan.

She arrived at her room and rushed inside, throwing the lock behind her, her heart pounding in her chest. Carrie took a moment with her eyes closed to breathe in deeply and remind herself that she was safe–this time.

Thanks to Robert Crawford.

"Robert, I swear to God," Victor began, glaring at his liegeman. "I ought to fire you right here and now."

Robert cleared his throat, not sure how to respond to the threats Victor was making–once again. He'd come up onto the deck looking for his employer because he'd gotten an important message he knew Mr. Anderson was waiting for. But when he'd discovered the situation with Miss Boxhall, he quickly realized he'd misread the situation the day before. When Carrie had sent him away, it wasn't because she wanted to be with Victor; she'd simply wanted to spare Robert from getting into trouble.

Here he was, facing that possibility again, and he had to admit, he didn't care. It was no secret to anyone that knew him well that Victor was a womanizer. As far as Robert knew, none of the women he'd been with in the past had been taken advantage of, but after over-hearing the conversation between Carrie and him, now he wasn't so sure.

One thing he did know for certain. There was nothing in the world more important than making sure that Carrie was safe and comfortable. Even if it cost him his employment, Robert wouldn't let Victor–or anyone–harm her.

"Mr. Anderson, I'm not exactly sure what was going on, but I distinctly heard Carrie tell you to leave her alone. You insisted on trying to take her back to your room, even though she didn't want that." Saying the words out loud made Robert even more angry than he had been before. It wasn't like him to be rude or aggressive, but in this case, he wasn't about to back down.

Victor stepped toward him, taking him roughly by the collar. "Listen here, boy. You answer to me. Don't you forget that. What happens between me and a dame–any dame–is none of your concern."

Robert yanked himself free, swiping Victor's arm away from him. His employer's eyes bulged in shock. "I am not a boy. I am a grown man. And regardless of the threats you make against me, I'm telling you right now, I will not put up with anyone threatening a woman–Carrie or anyone else."

"Do you want to find yourself sleeping out here on the deck?" Victor seethed, swiping his hand through his hair as his anger boiled to the surface.

Robert took a deep breath and looked around. Was he particularly excited about the possibility of being kicked out of his room? Of course not. But he wouldn't bow to Victor when he had done something so offensive. "Would you like to iron your own suits and fetch your own messages?" he countered. "I find it very unlikely you can find someone to replace me while we're situated out in the middle of the Atlantic."

Victor's eyes narrowed as he considered what Robert was saying. It was clear his liegeman had a point. Still, Victor was stubborn. "I'm Victor Anderson. I'll simply offer someone else's man more money. Who wouldn't rather work for me?"

Robert chuckled. "Are you sure you're willing to risk it?"

"Son of a bitch." Victor tugged at his hair again, swinging his arm by his side. "Go back to the room this instant and get it ready for me."

"No." Robert raised his head, his chin up, like his father had always told him. "I'm still considering whether or not I can work for someone like you."

Growling, Victor took a step toward him, lifting a finger and wagging it in his face. "If you're not back in the room in fifteen minutes, you're fired. I'll throw your shit out into the hallway, and you can sleep out here!" With that, he stormed off, still cursing under his breath.

Robert inhaled deeply and turned to the railing, resting his arms on the barrier and breathing in the sea air. His heart rattled against his ribcage. No matter how hard he told himself to calm down, nothing seemed to make a difference. He'd managed to stay in control while Victor berated him, but now, he felt himself coming apart. Was he willing to risk his job for a woman he hadn't seen in years?

The image of Carrie's face flickered before his eyes, and he knew for a fact that he was. Not just for Carrie, though. For too long, he'd looked the other way while Victor was out womanizing. Well, it was time he took a stand.

Robert felt himself beginning to grow more calm as his decision became more resolute. He turned and looked around the deck, noting that the chairs didn't look all that comfortable, but if he had to sleep out here beneath a blanket of stars for a day or two, it would certainly be worth it.

He heard the sound of a loud exhale and heavy steps and looked up in time to see Jonathan Lane tearing through a door. He knew Jonathan worked for the Ashtons, the same fine people that Carrie worked for, so he wasn't too surprised to see him here, but Jonathan looked out of sorts, which was unusual for him.

"Is everything well, Mr. Lane?" he called as Jonathan looked around the boat deck. "Are you looking for Miss Boxhall?"

Jonathan squinted at him, and realizing he was covered in shadows, Robert stepped into the light. A flicker of recognition crossed the other man's face as Jonathan stepped over. "Oh, Robert. It's you. Hello. Yes, I am looking for her. I was supposed to escort her back to the room if… well, I suppose I missed her." He lifted his signature hat and brushed his dark hair back.

Robert understood what Jonathan was not saying. He must've gone to the smoking lounge and intended to come and find Carrie if

Victor wasn't present. Clearly, Victor wasn't in the lounge, though he might be now, and Jonathan, who held himself to a high standard, slipped up.

"She went back to her room," Robert explained, moving back a few steps to hold onto the railing. He felt himself growing more tense with every word that left his mouth. "I came upon her in a bit of a tussle with Victor Anderson and insisted that he leave her be."

Jonathan's eyes practically bulged from his head. "A tussle? Was she harmed?"

"No, she wasn't harmed." Robert didn't think she was anyway. Now, he wished he would've gone with her, escorted her to her room, just to make sure she wasn't hurt in any way and that she got there safely. Who would've ever thought it would be unsafe for a woman to walk alone at night aboard a passenger liner? "I made sure that Victor knew, in no uncertain terms, that he must leave her alone."

Jonathan shook his head rapidly, his hands balling into fists. "That asshole. That perverted jackass. I have a mind to go find him and ram my fist so far through his nose he'll be smelling yesterday's flowers."

Robert bit off a chuckle, thinking now wasn't the time to laugh, even though the image of his employer–or was it former employer?-- with a bloodied nose was amusing to him. "I don't believe there's any need for that, Mr. Lane," Robert assured him. "I think I got my point across."

"But… you're his man," he reminded Robert, as if he might've forgotten. "Didn't he see fit to relieve you of your duties?"

"That's right," Robert confessed. "He did at first, but then it occurred to him that it might be difficult for him to replace me in the middle of the Atlantic, so he thought better of it. Still, I haven't decided what I want to do yet. While I most certainly don't want to work another minute for such an arrogant bastard, I'm not quite certain what I'll do. Those deck chairs don't look particularly comfortable, and I don't think I have enough money on me to afford anything except perhaps Third Class accommodations, if there are any available." He didn't make a habit of traveling with much money since his expenses were minimal while he was in service.

"Don't be ridiculous," Jonathan said with a laugh. "You're a friend of Carrie's, and any friend of Carrie's is a friend of mine. Not only did you step up to assist her, but I seem to recall the two of you had a real nice time at Mr. and Mrs. Ashton's wedding, didn't you?"

Robert felt his face heating. He hadn't been aware that anyone had noticed them dancing together at the wedding. But then, Carrie and Jonathan were close. Was it possible she mentioned it to him?

Was it possible she still thought about that night as often as he did?

Robert nodded. "Yes, Ms. Boxhall and I are friends. She's a wonderful woman. I couldn't imagine the likes of Victor Anderson getting his paws on her." Robert dragged a hand over his face, trying to clear his thoughts of what might've happened if he hadn't come along. Still, he wasn't sure what his friendship with Carrie had to do with him avoiding sleeping in an uncomfortable deck chair.

"Well, it's settled then." Jonathan clapped him on the arm. "You'll sleep on the couch in my room."

His mouth dropping open, Robert stared for a moment at Jonathan, not sure what to say. Finally, he managed, "That's a very generous offer of you, Mr. Lane, but I don't want to be any trouble."

"It's Jonathan," he corrected, tugging on his arm. "And it's no trouble whatsoever. I'm sure that Carrie would do the same for me if the circumstances were reversed."

Not sure what else to say, Robert offered his hand. "Thank you, Mr. La–Jonathan. I can't tell you how much I appreciate your hospitality."

Shaking his hand, Jonathan assured him, "It's no trouble at all. Now, come along. Let's get your things and head to the room."

9

Victor Anderson was running out of time to live.

At least, as Carrie got ready the next morning to go and join Jonathan for breakfast, as they had planned to do every morning while on the voyage, she couldn't help but think Victor Anderson may as well kiss this world goodbye. Once Jonathan found out what he'd done the night before, she was almost certain her friend would find a way to end him.

Oh, it probably wouldn't be so violent. No, Jonathan wasn't one to pull out a gun and shoot someone or even beat the living fire out of them. No, Jonathan would find a subtle way to help Victor along to the Promised Land—or in his case, probably a train in the totally other direction. He'd figure out a way to make Victor go bankrupt or something. Take away his money, and what did he have left?

"Not much," she muttered to herself while slipping her earrings into place. Carrie wasn't used to getting dressed like this on a daily basis, but it was kind of fun. Too bad she'd have to go back to wearing something much less fetching once this trip was over and she was just a lady's maid again.

As she finished making sure she was completely put together, she couldn't help but go over what had happened the night before. She'd been so startled after the incident with Victor, she'd just wanted to curl up in bed and hide. She'd heard Jonathan knock on her door a little while later, but she hadn't said anything, not until he'd called out, asking her if she was well. She'd assured him she was fine and just wanted to sleep, but now, well, now she'd have to face the music.

With a deep breath, she gave herself one more look in the mirror and then headed to the door that separated her room from Jonathan's. Once she told him what had happened, she was quite certain he'd lose his mind.

And then there was Robert. What had Victor done with poor Robert?

She knocked on the door but didn't wait for Jonathan to answer before stepping inside, and then–there was Robert!

Sitting on Jonathan's couch, looking as if he'd just woken up, the man who'd saved her the night before looked completely disheveled and out of sorts, as if he'd done something he couldn't quite come to terms with. He lifted his face in her direction, his dark eyes narrowing and then widening in recognition. "Carrie?"

"Robert?" Still shocked, she took a few steps inside of the room. "What are you doing here?"

Before he could reply, Jonathan walked out of his bedroom, buttoning up his shirt. Carrie stared at the pair of them for a moment, and only one thought came to mind. "Oh, my!" She took several quick steps backward and nearly ran into the door, which was still ajar. "Did you–"

"Carrie!" Jonathan's tone was stern as he shook his head at her. "You can't be serious! Do you really think I'd treat Edward that way?"

The shock of walking in on the two of them in such a state of undress melted away as she realized Jonathan was right. And it wasn't as if he'd been out there in the living room with Robert. He'd been in the bedroom until he'd heard her voice.

Her cheeks began to burn as she tried to come up with some sort of an explanation as to why she'd jumped to such an awful conclusion, but all she could think to say was, "I'm sorry, Jonathan. Of course you wouldn't. I–"

"It's fine." He shook his head and turned around to walk back into the bedroom. "I know you've had quite the evening." He closed the door behind him, which was a sign to Carrie that it wasn't quite fine, but he'd be all right once he had a moment to cool down.

Robert ran a hand through his hair and reached for his own jacket. "Who's Edward?"

"Uhm…." Carrie's mouth hung open for a moment as she tried to figure out a way to answer that question without saying more than she should. "He's… uhm…." She couldn't come up with anything so she decided not to answer at all. "Why are you here?"

"Oh, sorry." Robert stood, straightening his pants as he did so. "Mr. Lane said I could sleep on the couch since I ended my employment with Mr. Anderson."

Once again, Carrie found herself utterly stunned. "You did? You decided not to work for him anymore?"

"That's right. He gave me the opportunity to come back—after you left. But I couldn't bring myself to do it, not after learning what I did about how he treats women, particularly you. No, I've turned a blind eye toward Mr. Anderson for long enough."

Carrie wanted to tell him how noble that was, how much she admired his courage. It took a lot of gumption to quit one's job for any reason, but before she could get the words out, there was a knock at the door and a call of, "Room service!"

Jonathan stepped out of his room, looking totally put together now, and went to the door to let the man with the cart inside. "I ordered us some breakfast," he explained as he slipped the servant a few bills. The jolly chap left with a big grin on his face, thankful for Jonathan's generosity.

"That was very thoughtful of you." Carrie smiled, hoping he wasn't still angry at her. He seemed to have let it go as he returned the smile and gestured for her to sit down.

Robert waited for Carrie to take her seat and then sat back down on what must've been his bed the night before. It had to have been uncomfortable for a man of his height to sleep on a small couch, but then, she couldn't imagine where else he might've slept if he was no longer in Mr. Anderson's employment. The idea of Robert sleeping outside on a deck chair made her wince.

"Are you well?" he asked. Jonathan was busy setting their breakfast up outside where they could smell the fresh air, leaving them alone.

Carrie looked in her friend's direction, thinking perhaps she should offer to help, but she was glad for the time with Robert alone. "I'm fine, thank you. I was just thinking about how horribly uncomfortable that couch must've been."

"Oh, it wasn't that bad," he said with a smile and a slight shrug. "I've slept on worse."

Images of Robert in bed made Carrie's cheeks heat up. She found herself looking away just in time to see Jonathan gesturing for them to come join him.

As Carrie stood, so did Robert, drawing them so close together, they almost collided. She reached out a hand to steady herself, wrapping her fingers loosely around his arm.

His deep brown eyes enlarged only slightly as he took her in. "Pardon me." His voice was almost a whisper.

Not sure what to say, Carrie only smiled back at him, trying to slow the jagged breath that threatened to pour out of her, giving her predicament away. Being so close to him made her heart lose a steady rhythm.

"Are you coming?" Jonathan called in a playful voice. "Or shall I eat all of this by myself?"

"Coming, coming," Carrie assured him. Turning to go, she reluctantly let go of Robert's arm and felt the warmth drain from her fingers. How marvelous it would've been to have license to hold onto that strong arm whenever she wanted to.

Out on the deck, the breeze smelled of fresh salt air. The sun's golden rays painted the sky as the orb began to make its way toward a brilliant blue dome above them. Hardly a cloud dotted the heavens as Carrie looked out over the railing and took it all in.

"Today might be a fine day for Hannah to find some dolphins," Jonathan mused as he pulled Carrie's seat out for her. "The water's clearer here."

"Who is Hannah?" Robert asked as he took his seat next to Carrie.

"A girl we met recently," she explained. The men waited for her to serve herself. She took a spoonful of eggs, followed by some toast and a bit of bacon, but she wasn't all that hungry. Being this close to Robert had her stomach twisting in knots.

"She's on her way to boarding school," Jonathan continued. "It's a sad story really. Her parents were just killed in an automobile accident."

"That is terrible," Robert agreed as he placed some eggs on his plate. "Poor girl."

"We struck up a bit of a friendship with her." Carrie poked at her eggs, moving them around slightly on her plate. She realized she'd forgotten to pour her coffee and reached to do so just as Robert took the carafe. He smiled at her and filled her cup before filling his own, and once again, Carrie felt herself transforming into a bundle of vibrating nerves.

"It's lovely to make friends aboard the ship," Robert said, adding some cream to his coffee. "Or to find old ones."

"We haven't seen you since the wedding, I don't believe," Jonathan surmised. "How have things been—other than having to work for Anderson?"

Robert grumbled a bit at the mention of Victor's name. "I've been managing," he replied. "I've honestly been considering leaving his employment for some time now, so perhaps this is a blessing in disguise."

"I do appreciate you taking up for me last night." Carrie wasn't even sure if she'd properly thanked Robert for intervening. "I'm not sure what I would've done if no one would've stepped in."

"Of course." He kept his eyes on his plate as he scooped some eggs on his fork. She thought perhaps looking at her made him nervous as well. "I'm glad I was able to help."

"Miserable filth," Jonathan muttered. "He's lucky it wasn't me who'd come upon the scene. I would've given him an introduction to the cool water of the Atlantic he would've never forgotten."

"I'm glad you didn't come across us, too, then," Carrie replied, buttering a slice of toast she didn't intend to eat. "I'd hate for you to be in any sort of trouble."

Jonathan said nothing in response, only took a sip of his coffee. Carrie could tell he was still stewing on the situation. She wanted to ask him how it was he didn't get there first since he'd promised to come right out of the smoking lounge if Victor wasn't in there, but she didn't see the point in bringing it up now.

Instead, she decided on a happier subject. "What do you think you'll be doing now, Robert? Since you won't be in Mr. Anderson's employment anymore, will you be looking for work?"

Before Robert could answer, Jonathan offered, "I'm quite certain Mr. Ashton will provide you with employment, if you'd like."

"Thank you," Robert said, looking at Jonathan with a sincere smile. For a moment, Carrie imagined what it would be like to work in the same household as Robert. Would she be able to concentrate on any of her duties, or would she be too anxious all the time, too preoccupied with staring at the handsome gentleman? "But I actually think I may go into business for myself."

"Really?" Carrie was interested to hear more. "Doing what?"

"Well, I've been working on an idea for a while that has to do with improving the engine on an automobile. I've got some money saved up. Now is as good a time as any to see if I can be a success."

"You know, Mr. Ashton might be interested in hearing your plans. He's always been interested in automobiles," Jonathan said before finishing his last bite of eggs and wiping his mouth.

"I would love to speak to him about it." Robert set his napkin aside as if he, too, were finished, although he'd hardly taken a bite. Turning to Carrie, he asked, "What are your plans for today?"

Her mouth moved for a moment without making a sound before she managed to say, "I haven't any."

"Would you care to join me for some fresh air?" Those brown eyes stayed focused on hers, and Carrie could feel her pulse increasing again.

"Of course."

10

The warm sea breeze fluttered across Carrie's creamy skin, mixing with the floral scent of the perfume she wore, leaving Robert in a dizzy state he wasn't used to. Ordinarily, he had no trouble keeping his head on straight, but around this beautiful woman, he wasn't quite himself.

"The ocean is so beautiful today." Carrie held her hat tight in her hands. She'd intended to wear it, but even with the pins she'd placed, the wind was too much for it, so she'd taken it off a few moments ago and held it in her grasp. For a moment, Robert let himself think about what it would feel like to have those slender fingers wrapped tightly around his own hand. "Don't you think?"

Realizing she'd been speaking to him, he looked up into her eyes for a moment, replaying what she might've said. Something about the ocean... "Oh, yes. I agree." He hoped that made sense.

She let out a little giggle. "Are you all right, Robert?"

"I'm fine, thank you. Just... thinking about the situation with Victor." It wasn't the truth, but he could hardly tell her he was daydreaming about holding her hand.

"Were you able to collect your things from the cabin?" A concerned look slipped into place on her pretty face.

"Some of them." He nodded. "But I didn't take too long because I was afraid he'd come back from the smoking lounge and either start a fight or try to convince me, again, to continue to work for him."

"I'm sure he's a mess this morning." Again, the tinkle of her laughter rang out. He liked the sound of it even more than he did the noise of the ocean wrestling around the ship. "He probably doesn't even have his coat buttoned properly."

"I think he'll manage," Robert admitted, though it would be nice to think of his previous employer walking around the boat looking a mess because of his poor choices. "At any rate, I won't be going back to work for him now."

"I should think not. I love the idea you have for improving motor-coach engines, and I think it's wonderful that you've saved up some money. That's very responsible of you. In all of my years of working for the Ashtons, they've paid me very well, but I'm afraid I've never been frugal enough to save up too much."

"What do you prefer to do with your money?" Robert asked, doing his best not to sound judgmental. Not everyone was good at putting pennies back for a rainy day.

"Well, I do love to buy some of the nice clothing and shoes I see in the shops when I'm out with Mrs. Ashton," Carrie admitted. "Though I never spend too much on any one item. Honestly, I've been sending money home to my folks, and since my parents have gotten a little older, I know they've slowed down a bit on the farm, so I've been sending a little more than I used to." She sucked her bottom lip into her mouth and worked it between her teeth. Robert found himself leaning toward her, imagining how it would feel to have that same lip pressed against his. "I know my mother would rather I kept the money for myself, but I can't bear to think of them not being able to take care of themselves."

"That's very noble of you," Robert managed to say while still staring at her lip. He cleared his throat. "I think that's a perfectly good way to spend your money. Besides, you're perfectly happy with your employers, aren't you? No reason to think you may need to find another place to work or anything of that nature?"

"Oh, I love them like they're my own family," Carrie replied. For a moment, she reached out and placed her hand on his arm for emphasis before pulling it away, her fingers curling as she pressed the same hand to her shoulder. She made a little noise in the back of her throat that made him think she was concerned that she might've overstepped. He wished she would've touched him longer. "I can't imagine ever going anywhere else." As she turned away from him to face the ocean she added in almost a whisper, "Unless I were to marry."

Robert stood silently behind her for a moment contemplating that last remark. Why would she feel the need to be secretive about her wish to marry someday? Didn't all women want the same thing? To find a man who treated her with kindness and wanted to make her his wife?

Not sure of her reasoning for implying it was a secret, he let it go for the moment and stepped up next to her.

"I don't see any dolphins. Do you?" she asked as if they should be swimming around beside them like *Lusitania's* personal guard.

"No, I don't see any at the moment," he confirmed. "Have you seen any on our voyage?"

"One or two. At least, I think I did. Hannah said she saw several, though I thought it might've just been the way the waves look when shadows linger on them. It is hard to tell, you know?" She giggled again, and he laughed along with her.

"I suppose sometimes it is difficult to tell what you're looking at, but at other times, I think it can be crystal clear." When Robert looked at Carrie, he saw a beautiful, intelligent, kind woman.

The kind of woman he could see spending the rest of his life with, if he was honest.

He was just about to ask her another question, something more intimate, when he heard familiar footsteps and braced himself. "There you are. My shirt is a wrinkled mess. I need you to go iron it right away."

Victor approached them through the crowd of people walking along the promenade, straightening his cufflinks and carrying his jacket over one arm. Robert watched as his eyes bobbed to Carrie, and then returned to meet Robert's gaze.

Amusement bubbled up inside of him as he took a look at his former employer. Victor was wearing the same shirt he had on the day before, and while it was likely not as wrinkled as the shirt he'd planned to wear that day, it didn't look polished at all. And Victor Anderson always wanted to look polished.

Well, he was just going to have to figure out how to iron for himself.

"Excuse me?" Robert said, doing his best haughty impression. He'd heard quite a few men who were full of themselves over the years of working for Victor. "I should say not."

Victor's eyes bulged as he glanced from Robert to Carrie and then back again, as if he thought Carrie might take up for him. "What's that now? Robert Crawford, now you listen to me. You work for me, if you haven't forgotten."

"I do believe our employment arrangement was terminated last night." Robert stood tall. "And I don't intend to change that any time soon."

Huffing, Victor tapped his foot on the promenade. "Robert, listen. I need your help. I can't go mucking about like some sort of uncivilized… barbarian."

Robert opened his mouth to respond but found himself laughing, not at Victor's statement so much as the cute little snort and giggle Carrie let out as she covered her mouth with one hand and tried to disguise her amusement.

"It's not funny!" Victor shouted at Robert. "Come back to the room, and let us discuss this properly. You've left a good deal of your belongings behind. I figured, as soon as you were done with your… visit with Miss Boxhall, you'd come back to your duties."

All sense of amusement vanished from Robert's mind as he took in what Victor was implying. "I'll have you know I slept on the couch in Mr. Jonathan Lane's room last night, thank you very much, Mr. Anderson. And Ms. Boxhall didn't even know I was there."

Victor made a face, squeezing his lips together to one side of his mouth, as if he didn't buy it, which made Robert want to thump him into the ground even more. "Very well then, I apologize." In all the years that Robert had known him, he couldn't remember once ever hearing Victor say he was sorry for anything. "Now, please, just come with me."

"Give me a moment." Running a hand through his hair, Robert turned to Carrie, trying to determine what he should do.

"Perhaps you should hear him out?" She shrugged, and it was clear to him that she didn't mean the words at all. She'd thought so highly of him venturing out on his own. He hated to disappoint her now.

Besides, he agreed that he should start working for himself. The confidence it gave him when he spoke about his new invention, the way that Carrie and Jonathan both looked at him as if he had the capability of being someone important, the independence he found in that whisper of a dream—all of it was enough for him to know before he even excused himself from Carrie and followed Victor toward his First Class stateroom that he wouldn't be accepting his prior position back—no matter what.

Victor muttered under his breath as they headed down the narrow hallways. Every time they passed someone he knew, he was polite, and as soon as they were gone, he'd complain about his appearance. "I look like I'm the one who slept on a deck chair."

Clearing his throat, Robert bit his tongue. He hadn't slept on a deck chair, thanks to the good people he now counted as friends. He'd been lucky in that regard.

When they reached the room, Victor burst through the door and immediately started giving orders. "Iron that shirt first, and for the love of God, get that scuff off my shoes. I can't be seen wearing those at dinner tonight with that ridiculous mark all down the side."

Robert stared at him for a moment, watching as his former employer walked over to the table and poured himself a brandy—before lunch. Rather than obliging him with his orders, he began to gather up the belongings he'd left in the room. It wasn't much as most of his things were in his own sleeping area, and he'd gathered that the night before, but there were a few things lying about, like the brush he used to polish Victor's shoes. That had once belonged to his father.

He also found a telegraph from his mother he'd accidentally set aside the day before. She'd wished him a pleasant journey. Well, he'd have a lot to tell her when he returned home. He shoved that in his pocket and began to walk toward the door.

Looking up from the newspaper he was now reading, Victor asked, "Where are you going?"

"Away from you." Robert shrugged, not knowing how else to put it. "I already told you I don't want to work for you anymore."

"What? You have to." Victor slammed the paper down. "Who else will do all of the things I don't want to do?"

Chuckling under his breath, Robert said, "I don't give a damn."

"But—I won't be able to replace you until we reach shore. Maybe not even then. I'll pay you twice your salary."

That offer might've been tempting if Victor paid what he could afford in the first place—but he didn't. Opening the door, Robert stepped out into the hallway. "Good luck to you, Mr. Anderson."

As he closed the door and headed back toward Mr. Lane's room, he heard Victor shouting after him, calling him every name in the book. With a smile on his face, Robert just kept right on walking.

11

"Are you feeling all right, Miss Carrie?"

The sound of Hannah's voice brought Carrie out of a daze. How long had she been staring out at the ocean, thinking about Robert? She couldn't say, but she hoped she'd see him again soon. Surely, he hadn't decided to go back into service for the likes of Victor Anderson. When she'd suggested to Robert that he hear his former employer out, she hadn't hoped that he would actually take the job back. She'd only been trying to be diplomatic.

Not that Victor Anderson deserved such respect.

"I'm just fine, Hannah." Carrie managed a smile, which wasn't too hard as she looked down at the young lady. "I've just been looking for dolphins again, that's all." It wasn't exactly a lie. She'd been staring out at the ocean hard enough that she might've seen a dolphin if any wandered by, though it might not have registered since she was so lost in her thoughts.

Hannah took hold of the railing next to her. "I heard a rumor at lunch yesterday. Quite a scary one."

Carrie arched an eyebrow and looked over at her as she rocked back and forth from the tips of her toes to her heels, unable to stand completely still, which seemed to be the case for most young people, in her experience. "And what was that?" Carrie couldn't help but ask, even though she wasn't sure she wanted to know.

"I heard a gentleman saying that the Germans are going to send a big, explosive torpedo right into the heart of this very ship, and it will rip *Lusitania* right in half. All of us will either be blown to bits or fall into the ocean." Hannah spoke with such enthusiasm, it was as if she were telling a tale from a storybook, not retelling one man's interpretation of what might happen if the newspapers were correct and the Germans did send a torpedo at their passenger liner.

"Oh, well, I really don't think that's something we need to worry about." Carrie caught the eyes of Hannah's governess, who was sitting in a deck chair nearby, close enough to hear Hannah's energetic voice. She only rolled her eyes and opened the book she held in her hand. "I think we will be just fine."

"Do you think so?" Hannah moved down the railing a little bit, her eyes peering out at the ocean. Now, Carrie wasn't sure if she was looking for dolphins–or torpedoes. They were still too far out into the Atlantic for that, Carrie assumed. At least, she hoped so.

"Yes, I do think so," Carrie reassured her. "I'm not worried in the least."

"About what now?" Jonathan came up behind Hannah and tugged on one of her pigtails, making the girl laugh. "Are you looking for an enormous whale out there, one big enough to pick this ship up out of the water and swallow it down whole?"

"Like Jonah?" Hannah asked with a giggle. "No, we were talking about the torpedoes, that's all."

Jonathan gave Carrie a quizzical look that morphed into something a bit more sinister.

"It's nothing really. Only some silly man talking at lunch," Carrie assured him.

Jonathan nodded. "That's right. I'm sure everything will be just fine. If something were to go wrong, well this ship has plenty of lifeboats. You've seen them, during the drills."

"Yes, I did see them, but I've never been inside one before. Have you?" Hannah's eyes were wide with curiosity as she stared into Jonathan's face.

Carrie saw the silent shutter that went down his spine as his eyes stayed placid, almost as if he'd slipped into a trance for a moment. She could only imagine the visions that sprang before his eyes.

After a moment, he cleared his throat and nodded. "I have been in one before."

Hannah gasped and covered her mouth with both hands. "What happened? Was it a terrible wreck at sea? Did your boat collide with another ship?"

"No, no, nothing like that." It was clear he was trying to play down the ordeal. Carrie knew how he hated to talk about *Titanic* almost as much as Charlie and Meg. "It was just a bit of a problem with the ship, that's all. We got on the lifeboats, another ship came, and we got off. Simple as that."

"Oh, that must've been so exciting." Hannah clasped her hands together.

"Well, at least she's not frightened," Carrie mused under her breath. She'd thought she'd have to talk the girl out of worrying about a torpedo causing a problem, but now it seemed she was actually hoping for a bit of excitement. Unusual, considering her parents' demise, but then, Hannah was a world traveler. Perhaps that was part of the fun for her, looking for the next adventure.

"How long did you have to get aboard the lifeboat before the ship sank?" Hannah asked Jonathan, still clasping her hands before her.

Eighteen minutes...

Ruth's voice echoed through Carrie's head, and that spine-tingling sensation she'd imagined her friend experiencing only a few minutes ago sent her heart racing. No, that was silly. Of course, Ruth couldn't predict something like that.

"We had a couple of hours," Jonathan replied, his tone nonchalant, as if he'd just leisurely strolled over to a lifeboat, got in, and sailed across the ocean to a waiting *Carpathia*. "No, I really don't think it's a matter to concern ourselves over in the least."

"Can we go look at the lifeboats?" Hannah pleaded, practically bouncing up and down.

"If it's all right with your governess." Jonathan turned to look at Mrs. Smythe who gave a dismissive wave of her hand. Hannah squealed in delight, and Carrie took her hand to walk the short distance to the closest lifeboats. She imagined it would be a good idea for her to listen to Jonathan talk about them as well since she had been a bit distracted during the muster.

For about thirty minutes, Jonathan talked to both of them about how lifeboats operated, what was in them, what to do if they should ever find themselves in one, and why it was important to keep a level head on one's shoulders when faced with an emergency. All Hannah could talk about was how exciting it would be to ride the large waves of the Atlantic in such a tiny boat.

Something else Ruth had done came to mind and made Carrie ask a question before giving it too much thought. "What happens if the boat is listing?" Visions of Ruth holding that train, making an exploding sound, filled her mind.

Jonathan lifted his face toward hers. "What do you mean?"

Thinking perhaps she shouldn't ask such daunting questions in front of Hannah, Carrie considered dropping it, but the girl was walking around the lifeboat, running her hand along the outer surface, clearly lost in a daydream where she was coasting along the top of white-tipped waves out on the open ocean.

"I mean," Carrie began, keeping her voice down. Jonathan walked a few steps closer. "If something traumatic did happen to *Lusitania,* or a different boat, were to be... severely injured, how would the lifeboats manage to get off without... tipping?"

"Tipping?" Jonathan dragged a hand down his jaw, his eyes wandering over the mechanisms that lowered the boats into the ocean, the boat itself, and then over the side of *Lusitania.* Finally, he shook his head. "I'm honestly not exactly sure, Carrie. If the boat was listing that badly before the lifeboats could get off, well, there probably wouldn't be too many people even capable of getting in them. The lowering system is sound. It should be able to do the trick under most circumstances–if the crew acts quickly."

Carrie nodded, swallowing hard. He had basically told her that if a torpedo hit the ship hard enough to make it list before the boats got away, there wouldn't be anyone left to get into the boats. It was a sobering thought.

"Hannah!"

Mrs. Smythe's voice cut through her negative thoughts. All three of them turned to see the governess standing about ten feet away, beckoning with her arm.

Hannah let out a sigh. "I don't know why we have to go in so early. I'd much rather visit with the pair of you than go back to the room and watch Mrs. Smythe read a book."

As she passed by, Carrie ran a hand lovingly along her shoulder. "Maybe you could read a book?"

"Maybe." Hannah let out another breath. "See you both tomorrow?"

"I hope so." Jonathan's cheerful smile brightened Hannah's face–until she turned around to look at her governess, and her shoulders sagged again.

"That one… I do feel sorry for her sometimes." He shook his head, shoving his hands deep into his pants pockets and rocking back and forth in the ocean breeze.

"I do, too." Carrie watched Hannah and her governess walk away, hoping everything worked out well for the poor girl. Then, she turned to Jonathan and asked a question she wasn't sure she wanted to hear the answer to. "Did Ruth know?"

He raised an eyebrow as his eyes fell on her face, as if he was trying to work out what she wasn't saying in the vague question. It only took him a moment to work it out, though. Nodding his head, he walked a few steps away from the lifeboat. Carrie followed. "I think she may have."

A chill ran its way down the length of Carrie's spine. "I've heard her say some odd things over the years. Like telling Henry it'll only hurt for a minute a few seconds before he bonked his head or saying she'll get a towel before her mother spilled her tea on her gown."

He chuckled, but she could still see the shadow behind his eyes. "I never heard her say anything specific last time, but later, her mother and Meg both mentioned that she'd said something about getting on a new boat, and something else about God being able to sink that ship."

Carrie noted he wouldn't even say the name–*Titanic*. "Well, I hope she was just being silly this time. I'd hate to think…." Now, she was the one who couldn't speak.

"What did she say?" Jonathan turned toward her, even more concern in his expression now.

She studied him for a second, noted how the fine lines around his eyes and nose were more defined when he was worried.

"She said this time we'd only have eighteen minutes–and she made an exploding sound. She tipped this toy train at an odd angle. I honestly don't know, Jonathan. She's a little girl who was playing with toys at the time." Carrie forced a laugh. "Children have such vivid imaginations."

"That they do." He nodded. "That they do." After a moment of awkward silence, he cleared his throat. "Well, I think we'll arrive just fine, but if something happens, we just have to trust that our time comes when it's meant to."

While she didn't particularly like the thought of that either, Carrie found herself nodding along.

"Now, I have an idea." His smile brightened his whole face, making him look years younger.

"What's that?" She couldn't help but smile back at him.

"I know you're not a fan of the First Class dining room, and since Robert isn't allowed to eat there, why don't the two of you dine in the room? I'll arrange it."

Excitement bubbled up inside of Carrie, and she felt like Hannah had at the notion of seeing the lifeboats. "Really? You can do that?"

He laughed. "I can do anything."

She knew that to be true. Not worried one bit about whether or not it was appropriate, she said, "That would be lovely." Thoughts of spending the evening in Robert's company had her practically giddy.

Whatever would she wear?

12

"You look lovely, Carrie," Jonathan assured her. For the hundredth time since she'd finished dressing, she checked herself in the mirror. He'd come over a few moments before he needed to leave for dinner in the dining hall to see if she needed anything. Thankfully, he didn't flinch when she asked him to help her with a few buttons on her gown she couldn't quite reach. Sometimes it paid to have a male friend who wasn't interested in women.

"Thank you." Carrie turned to smile at him. "I am a bit nervous."

A crooked grin took over Jonathan's face. "I knew there was something between you, even if neither of you would admit it. Initially, I thought it would be a good idea for you to stay out of the dining hall because of Victor, but now I see that this is a more suitable arrangement for other reasons as well."

"Oh, stop!" Carrie brushed her hand over his arm dismissively. "It's nothing like that."

"Please. You sound like Charlie trying to deny he was interested in Meg a few nights into our embarkment on the ship that won't be named." He shook his head and took a few steps toward the door. "I doubt I'll go to the smoking lounge tonight. I don't want to see Victor."

"Can't fault you there," Carrie muttered.

"Behave yourself, Miss Boxhall. I'd hate to have to tell your employer you've become a temptress."

He was almost to the door, so he was out of reach for her to smack him upside the head. Instead, Carrie picked up a glove she'd considered wearing and tossed it at him. She missed, and they both laughed before he disappeared through the door.

"That Jonathan." Mumbling to herself, she crossed the room and picked up the glove. In the time it took her to walk back over to the table to set it down, she found herself second guessing her choice. Should she switch the ones she was wearing for the others?

A knock on the door between her room and Jonathan's made all other thoughts disappear from her mind. That would be Robert letting her know dinner had been delivered. Carrie sucked in a deep breath and dropped the now-forgotten glove on the table.

Her stomach tangled in a knot of nerves, she pulled open the door and smiled at Robert, hoping he couldn't tell how anxious she truly felt about dining with him. His warm brown eyes met hers, and she felt herself begin to breathe naturally again.

"Good evening, Miss Carrie," he said politely, stepping back out of her way and gesturing for her to come in. "You look stunning."

Instinctively, Carrie looked down at her gown, as if she'd forgotten what she was wearing. This dress was also new, though she wished she had saved the one she liked better for an occasion such as this one. Not that she ever would've guessed she'd be dining–alone–with Robert Crawford.

"Thank you." She tugged at the train of the green gown which highlighted her eyes. "I bought it just before we left."

"The gown is very nice, but I meant you, Carrie. Not your dress or the fancy pins you have in your hair or the jewels dripping from your earlobes and adorning your neck." His voice was smoky, as if he'd just awoken from a dream–a dream about her.

Carrie felt the air leaving her lungs again, but this time, it was for a different reason entirely. Not knowing what to say, she simply stared at his handsome face for a moment, noticing the squareness of his clean-shaven jaw, the way his nose was perfectly straight, how his eyebrows arched when he was amused.

"Shall we?" He broke the silence, taking a few steps toward a table that had been set up in the middle of the lounge area and pulling out a chair. "I thought it would be safer to dine in here since the sea is a bit turbulent this evening. Wouldn't want to end up with a lap full of prime rib."

Giggling, Carrie took the offered seat and waited for Robert to take the chair across from her before placing her napkin in her lap. It was an intimate setting with barely enough room for their plates and drinks. Removing the cloches did help. Robert discarded them and poured them both a glass of wine. Before she could pick up her fork, he raised his glass. "To dinner with the most interesting individual on the ship."

Heat rose in Carrie's cheeks as she clinked her glass against his. "To finding an old friend under new circumstances." She held his gaze for a moment, wondering if he would understand exactly what she was getting at.

His smile widened, and she assumed he did.

The two of them began their meal with polite conversation about the weather and Jonathan's lovely idea that she should skip the dining hall, but soon, the topic of conversation became deeper. "Do you like working for Mrs. Ashton?" Robert asked her before taking a sip of his wine.

Carrie nodded. "Yes, of course. I love them like they are my own family."

"And do you see yourself in their employment for the rest of your days?" That hint of amusement she noticed quite often colored his expression as he waited for her response.

Only a few days ago, Carrie would've been quick to say of course she did. But since then, her circumstances had changed. Now, she had had a taste of life on the ocean–in First Class–and Robert's willingness to step out on his own had also inspired her.

"I'm honestly not certain," she admitted after swallowing down a bite of steak. "I do love working for the Ashtons. But I'm not sure that's all I want out of life." Thoughts of what it would be like to marry, have children, a home of her own all flashed before her eyes. While it seemed ridiculous for Carrie to think about marrying Robert, she'd be lying to herself if she said the idea wasn't appealing. She picked up her glass of wine and took a drink to calm her nerves.

She was in the process of swallowing when Robert asked, "Do you want to get married?"

Choking on the wine, Carrie sputtered, spewing flecks of wine across the table, her lap, and Robert's plate.

Immediately, he handed her the napkin from his lap. "Are you all right?"

She coughed a few times and placed her glass down, taking the napkin and pressing it to her mouth. Thankfully, they were drinking white wine, so there were no stains on the tablecloth or her dress. "I'm so sorry." She wondered how much of it had actually gotten on his food and if he would continue to eat it after that.

Chuckling, he said, "It's fine, Carrie. You do realize I was asking if you'd get married someday in general–not proposing?"

Feeling heat rush to her face, Carrie forced herself to nod. Yes, of course he wasn't proposing. What was wrong with her anyway? "Oh, I know." She managed to eke out the response, but on the inside, she was still embarrassed from her reaction. If he had been asking her to marry him, he would've taken it back after that reaction.

"Good," he said, leaning toward her and lowering his voice. "Because if I were proposing, you'd know it."

A chill went down Carrie's spine, and for a moment, she allowed herself to stare into his eyes and think about what it would be like to press her lips against his.

When he leaned away from her, she caught her breath and looked away, knowing she needed to control herself. She wasn't the sort of woman Victor thought she might be, so she needed to get a handle on herself.

Robert cut another piece of steak and ate it as if he hadn't noticed the wine at all. She went back to her food and took a few more bites before he asked her a few more questions. What did she think of the ship? Did she enjoy traveling? What exactly was she doing for Mrs. Ashton in Southampton? Carrie answered all of his questions and asked a few of her own. He explained the mechanics behind his motorcoach improvements, though she didn't quite follow what he was saying. She'd never been particularly mechanically inclined.

"If you could do anything else, be anything else, what would you be?" he asked her, his steak nearly devoured.

Carrie didn't even have to think about that. "Honestly? I love fashion. When Mrs. Ashton and I go shopping, I love taking in all the newest styles. I don't have much time to sew anymore, but when I do, I like to see what I can create. I'm not sure I'm all that good at it, but I find it interesting."

"I'm sure you're a wonderful designer." He didn't hesitate to compliment her. "Do you think one day you might like to strike out and try your hand at it? As a profession?"

"I don't know." She hadn't really told anyone about her desire to create dresses and other articles of clothing. Not even Mrs. Ashton or Kelly. It seemed silly for a lady's maid to want to do something of that nature. "It's not like I'd ever have the money to do something like that."

"Why not try making a dress or two, see if those sell, and then you could make more?" he suggested. "Start small and work your way up."

She hadn't really thought about doing it that way. "The idea of opening a dress shop sounds overwhelming, but when you put it that way, it seems more manageable."

"Do you think the Ashtons would be willing to support you in such an endeavor?" Robert wiped his mouth and set his napkin back in his lap.

Shrugging, she admitted, "I've never really thought of asking them about something like that. Knowing Mr. Ashton, he would probably pay for the whole thing. He's very generous to his friends, and I'd like to think of myself as his friend. And then Mrs. Ashton has her own money as well. But I don't know. I'd sort of like to do it on my own."

He nodded, his lips curling into a soft smile. "I believe that. You seem quite independent."

Not knowing how to respond, Carrie took another bite of her steak. She was almost full, but she didn't want the meal to end. They continued to chat for a few more minutes while she got as much of the delicious dinner down as she could.

When they were finished eating, he asked, "Would you like to step out onto the balcony? I know how much you enjoy staring out at the sea." He gave her a knowing look that made her wonder if perhaps he'd been watching her when she didn't know it.

"Yes, I'd like that." The two of them pushed their chairs back and placed their napkins on the table before making their way out to the deck. A silver moon lit the waves as they rippled out from the speeding passenger ship. The soft breeze brushed through the loose tendrils of her hair. Carrie breathed it all in, resting her hands on the railing and reminding herself that this was real. She wasn't home in New York City, sitting in bed with her nose in a book. She was here on this magnificent ship, with a wonderful man standing only inches from her.

"You sure look lovely tonight, Carrie," he murmured, stepping even closer to her.

"Th-thank you." She looked up into his eyes, and that same spell that had fallen over her before rushed over her.

Robert slowly closed the distance between them, and Carrie pushed up on her tiptoes, her eyelashes fluttering closed. His lips were so close to hers, she could practically feel them on hers already.

"I'm back!"

The sound of Jonathan's voice had both of them leaping away from one another, Carrie biting back a curse she'd been about to let fly. Robert snickered and shook his head as Jonathan walked out onto the balcony.

"What?" he asked, completely oblivious to what he'd just interrupted.

Laughing, Carrie pressed a hand to her forehead. "Nothing, Mr. Lane. Wonderful timing as always. How was dinner?"

13

"Well? How was your evening last night? Did you enjoy the food?"

The clanking of silverware and dishes in the dining lounge mingled with Jonathan's quiet tone, making Carrie have to lean forward to hear him clearly. "It was delicious," she said, knowing that was likely not what he was fishing for. After he'd returned from the First Class Dining Lounge the night before, Carrie hadn't stuck around long. She'd known Robert had been about to kiss her but had stopped when Jonathan interrupted. While the liegeman didn't seem to catch on right away, he was an intelligent fellow and had realized his faux pas pretty quickly, though he hadn't said anything.

"That's good to know. And the company?" He took a bite of his chicken and waited patiently as Carrie felt her face flushing red.

"Robert is very kind. He's polite. The perfect gentleman." She lifted her glass to her lips and slowly took a sip of water.

A smirk pulled up one side of Jonathan's face. "Oh? Was he being a perfect gentleman when I walked in last night?"

Under the table, Carrie kicked Jonathan in the shin, not hard enough to hurt him. He laughed in response. "Stop. Don't tell me you've never kissed a woman on a date before." Jonathan arched an eyebrow and opened his mouth to correct her. "A person—rather." She rolled her eyes. "Have you ever… dated a woman?" Her question was a whisper so that no one would overhear. The dining area for breakfast and lunch was come and go and could get rather crowded sometimes, depending upon the time of day. Right now, the crowd was dense enough that most of the tables around them were occupied.

"I have," Jonathan confirmed. "And I believe you are changing the subject."

Carrie's mouth fell open as she considered arguing with him, but she couldn't, so she lifted her glass again.

"Thirsty?" He chuckled under his breath.

"I am thirsty, thank you very much." She shook her head and set her glass aside. "Listen, Robert and I have known each other for years. It's not as if we are mere strangers."

"I know that." He took another bite, unbothered by the distress he was causing her.

"And he was a perfect gentleman."

"I'm sure he was. I wouldn't have left you alone with him if I had any doubts."

"Well… I'm not your charge, you know." Carrie cut into her own meal, not even paying close enough attention to remember if she'd gotten the chicken or beef dish until she tasted the latter on her tongue. She chewed with a purpose. "You're here to keep me safe, not to help me make choices regarding my virtue."

Jonathan made a gesture with his head that was a mix between nodding in agreement and shaking it in difference. "I wouldn't want you to do anything compromising with a man you'll likely never see again."

"But you said yourself you thought Mr. Ashton could get him a job," she reminded him.

"True. Would that make it better or worse, though? If something happened between the pair of you that meant more to you than it did to him, and then you were faced with seeing him every few days?"

Carrie took a moment to dwell on those options before replying. "I rarely see the gentlemen that work for Mr. Ashton, other than yourself and Mr. O'Connell," she reminded him. The rest of the foremen and men who worked in the factory didn't ever come to the house.

"Still, Carrie, would you want to put yourself in that situation? Where you put yourself out there for someone who thinks that it's just a fun time for both of you?" Jonathan's eyes were full of sincerity and care for her.

"No, of course not." She didn't bother to tell him she'd done that before. It wasn't his business. "I do think there's a chance that Robert does truly care about me, though."

He nodded. "I think he might as well, but I would suggest you make sure before you leap without looking."

Before Carrie could say anything else, a young woman perhaps a bit older than her stopped next to their table, carrying a full tray of food. "I do beg your pardon," she said, "but all the tables are full. Would it be possible for me to join you?"

Jonathan lifted his head, and his eyebrows nearly touched one another. "Of course, you can. But... you look very familiar to me."

She set her tray down, and Jonathan, always the gentleman, pulled her chair out for her. "I thought you looked familiar as well. I'm Vivian Jenson."

Jonathan reclaimed his seat. "Yes, of course. I recognize you from the papers. I don't believe we ever met. Jonathan Lane." He offered her hand, and she took it.

Carrie watched, not sure how they knew one another until Vivian said, "Yes—you were with the Ashtons."

"I was traveling with them. I got off with Mrs. Ashton's lady's maid. She was, of course, Ms. Westmoreland at the time. What lifeboat were you in?" Jonathan asked.

"Sixteen," Ms. Jenson replied. Carrie noted both of them had a hazy look in their eyes. They had to be talking about *Titanic*, of course. It was more than she'd heard Jonathan say about it in quite some time.

"Ah, one of the first to leave the port side." Jonathan suddenly seemed as if he were reminiscing about something that happened when he was in grade school, a game of some sort, in Carrie's opinion, and it was fascinating to listen to the two of them chat about their experience without touching on anything too traumatic for either of them.

"That's right. We were out there for quite some time. Took forever for all the port boats to get to *Carpathia*." Vivian swallowed hard enough for Carrie to see her throat moving. "I don't generally talk about the events of that night." She straightened the tight white lace around her throat.

"Neither do I," Jonathan admitted. "Though from time to time, it is nice to meet a kindred spirit so we can remind one another that we survived."

Noting the gleam in his eyes Jonathan often got when he spoke of how lucky he had been to make it into a lifeboat when so many others hadn't, Carrie began to fidget with her napkin. She had so many questions she wished she had the opportunity to ask anyone who actually was willing to talk about what had happened, but no one she knew who'd been aboard ever liked to speak of it.

For a moment, she imagined what it would be like to float along inside a crowded lifeboat out in the open sea, at night, with no moon. It had to have been terrifying and invigorating at the same time. Of course, the others in the lifeboat might've been missing loved ones, praying for their spouses, etc. Carrie didn't have anyone like that in her life–a husband or children, so if she'd been in the boat, it would've been her friends she would've been praying for.

"Carrie?" Jonathan said her name in a manner that made her think it wasn't the first time he'd spoken. "Vivian just asked if we were planning to attend the Gretchen Flynn concert this evening."

"Oh?" Carrie felt her face flush as she realized she'd been paying absolutely no attention whatsoever to their conversation once the topic left *Titanic*. "I didn't realize there was a concert aboard the ship."

"Yes, Ms. Flynn is quite an accomplished singer, and she'll be gracing us with a performance this evening. I am hoping my husband is up and about and able to attend. He hasn't been feeling well. I think it's seasickness. Ever since *Titanic*...." Her voice trailed off, and Carrie let it go. She had wondered if the woman's husband was also a survivor, and now she knew. How remarkable that they had both made it out of the situation alive.

"I'm sorry to hear he's not feeling well." Carrie took another bite of her beef and swallowed it before saying, "I think a concert sounds lovely. What do you think?"

"I think… it would be a lovely way to spend an evening." He gave her a tight-lipped smile that made her think he was implying that perhaps she should attend the concert with someone else. Either that, or Carrie was simply getting away with herself. Thoughts of spending an evening with Robert sent a tingle up her spine and had her stomach tightening in knots. It would be so lovely to listen to some beautiful music while sitting right next to him. She wondered if he was the type of gentleman who might let a tear or two roll down his cheeks when a particularly moving melody hit him just right.

Realizing she was lost in a daydream again, she forced herself to tune into the conversation around her. Now, they were discussing other concerts each of them had attended in New York City, London, even Paris. Carrie was surprised to hear Jonathan had seen some of the most famous performers in the world perform at the most expensive venues. She wanted to ask if he'd always been there to accompany Mr. Ashton, but it didn't seem her place. If Mrs. Jenson was aware that they were both actually servants to wealthy people, she didn't let on. She treated them with the same sort of respect anyone else in First Class might deserve.

"What about you, Mrs. Lane?" Mrs. Jenson asked after a few minutes of just Jonathan sharing his favorite concert memories. "What's your favorite place to listen to music?"

"Oh, we're not–" Carrie looked at Jonathan and made an awkward motion. "We're just friends." She realized then she hadn't properly introduced herself. Offering her hand, she said, "Carrie Boxhall."

"I beg your pardon." Vivian's cheeks turned a little red. "I suppose I shouldn't have made assumptions."

"It's no trouble," Jonathan assured her. "We're traveling together to retrieve some items for Mrs. Ashton, whom you might know is about to have her second baby."

"I had read about that in the papers," Mrs. Jenson said with a nod.

Carrie jumped in to answer the question. "I haven't actually ever been to a concert before, other than just little bands around my small hometown growing up that used to play at fairs and the like. I've heard some street musicians before in New York, of course, and marching bands in a parade. But... this will be my first concert."

Vivian's face lit up. "Well, then you should make the most of it. Gretchen Flynn is delightful. It's a night I'm sure you'll never forget." She stood, gathering up her dishes. "It was a pleasure chatting with both of you. Take care."

With that, she stood and disappeared into the crowded room, and Carrie found herself letting out a deep breath.

"Is anything the matter?" Jonathan asked her. "It's not because she thought we were married?"

Laughing, Carrie patted his arm. "No, of course not. I could do worse, I tell you." That got a chuckle out of him. "I was just thinking perhaps she's right. Tonight could be a special evening."

With a knowing smile, Jonathan chuckled and said, "I'm sure I have no idea what's up your sleeve, Carrie Boxhall."

They gathered their belongings. "I'm sure you do."

14

Reading the newspaper was much more enjoyable when one was alone. Or, at the very least, it was much easier to concentrate when the only sounds Robert could hear were the lapping of the water against the hull of the ship as it sped through the water and the occasional footsteps of a fellow passenger walking by in the hallway.

How long had it been since he'd had the opportunity to sit and read a newspaper without having to drop it every few moments so that Victor could have more coffee or have a cigar handed to him or something else silly that he could've done himself? For that matter, most of the time, even if Victor wasn't demanding Robert perform some menial task, he was ranting and raving about something ridiculous, like how workers demanded a livable wage and how he had to pay taxes to support such worthless causes as schools for underprivileged children. "If a parent can't afford schooling, let their child get a job!" he'd once shouted when reading over a tax statement.

"How someone that cruel and selfish deserves to have that kind of money, I'll never understand," he muttered, finishing the business section and folding it before taking a sip of the coffee he'd poured himself with his own two capable hands.

His eyes went to the balcony where he'd shared a delightful

moment with Carrie the night before. She was so lovely, such a kind, intelligent woman. How lucky was he that she just happened to be on this same boat with him?

The situation had turned intimate the night before, and he'd been about to kiss her. In some ways, he was glad Jonathan had come back at the moment he did. While Robert longed to taste Carrie's lips to feel their soft warmth against his, he knew it wasn't respectable for him to kiss a lady he was only just getting reacquainted with. Some would argue the pair of them shouldn't have been having dinner unchaperoned, for that matter, and they might be right. Though certain exceptions were often made for working women, such as Carrie, Robert didn't see her as any less of a lady than the other women who held First Class status. For that matter, in Robert's opinion, there wasn't a finer lady in the world than Carrie Boxhall.

He took a deep breath. He was getting in deep. Whether that was a good thing or a bad thing, he couldn't say at present, but it seemed to him that Carrie was leaning in for a kiss, not leaning away.

He was just about to pick the newspaper back up when there was a sound at the door. The sound of Carrie's laughter filtered in, and he immediately smiled. Standing, he set the paper aside and greeted her as she came through the door with Jonathan. "Did the two of you enjoy your lunch?"

"We did," she said with a fond smile. Jonathan closed the door behind her, nodding in agreement. "It's a shame you couldn't come."

They had invited him, but he'd decided to give them some space and stay in the room. While he loved spending time with Carrie, he didn't want to overwhelm her. "I got caught up on all of the financial matters back in the city." He tapped the newspaper.

"Is that the one I brought on board with me?" Jonathan chuckled. "I suppose it's old news by now."

"Yes, well, it was all new to me." He laughed and placed his hands in the pockets of his slacks. It was too bad he only had his uniforms and one other outfit with him, which was nothing fancy. He felt out of place still dressed like a servant.

"We ate lunch with a lovely woman named Vivian Jenson," Carrie said as she came around to sit on the couch. Jonathan joined her, and Robert reclaimed his chair. "She told us about a concert that's going on this evening. Can you believe they're having a concert right here on the ship?"

Robert knew many ships offered entertainment to First Class passengers, not that he'd ever attended anything of the sort. "That's fascinating."

"Yes, and a very famous singer by the name of Gretchen Flynn is going to sing for us. Isn't that lovely?" Her face lit up when she spoke, so Robert could tell Carrie was excited by the idea.

"It does sound wonderful." He managed a smile, but his previous thoughts about his attire came back to him. Besides, he wasn't technically even a First Class passenger, so he probably shouldn't even consider attending.

Carrie cleared her throat. "Would you like to attend? Or do you have plans?"

"Oh, uhm, I'm not sure." Robert pursed his lips, trying to decide how to answer. It was as if she were asking him on a date. Even if that wasn't her intention, that's how he felt. By the look on her face, he could tell she thought he would decline. "It's only...." Robert gestured at his clothing. "I don't have anything proper to wear."

"That's not a problem," Jonathan said dismissively. "You're a bit taller than me, probably broader in the shoulders, but I think one of my suits will work."

"I can let it out," Carrie offered. "I'm not a seamstress by any means, but I know a thing or two."

"Do you think the other First Class passengers would mind if I were there?" Robert leaned in a bit as he spoke, as if he thought the others might somehow overhear from their luxurious rooms onboard.

"You'll go in my stead," Jonathan said with a shrug.

Carrie's eyes widened. "I thought you wanted to go."

"It's not so important to me. I'd rather the two of you went together and had a nice time. I can catch Gretchen the next time she comes to the city."

"Are you sure?" Robert asked just as Carrie clapped her hands in glee. Apparently, she was sure.

"That's wonderful," she gushed, squeezing Jonathan's arm. "You're simply the best, Jonathan Lane."

"I know." He wagged his eyebrows at her and stood, walking toward his bedroom. "I'll grab one of my suits for you."

While Robert knew Carrie and Jonathan were merely friends, a tinge of jealousy climbed the back of his neck at the way they interacted. He wished Carrie could be so playful with him. Maybe she would be one day, if he was lucky enough.

With Jonathan in the other room, Robert had the perfect opportunity to speak to Carrie alone. Yet, when he looked in her direction, his mind went blank. All he could think about was how lovely she was.

He could say that. He could tell her how she was beautiful, how he'd been picturing her face all day. He opened his mouth, thinking he'd say something dashing. "You sure look... full."

Carrie's mouth fell open as she stared at him. "I look... full?"

Robert ran a hand through his hair, cleared his throat, and gaped at her. "I mean... how was lunch?"

A giggle escaped her lips. "It was fine. I suppose you must mean the food since I look so full?"

"I didn't mean–" At a loss for words, Robert only shrugged. He'd fully meant to say she looked beautiful. It just hadn't come out right.

"I had the beef dish," she added. "It was a bit more chewy than I prefer, but it wasn't bad."

He nodded, trying to think of something to say to redeem himself. He hadn't eaten any lunch yet, so he couldn't tell her what he'd eaten.

"Here we are." Thankfully, Jonathan came out of his room with a suit, saving him from more embarrassment–at least temporarily.

Carrie hopped up off the couch, clapping her hands. "Wonderful!" She took the suit by the hanger and moved toward Robert. "Do you think this will work?"

Nodding, he stood. "I think so." He could tell it would be a bit too short and it might be tight in the shoulders, but he thought it would work.

Taking the jacket off the hanger, Carrie held it out for him. Realizing she wanted him to try it on, Robert slouched out of his work jacket and slid the other one on. As suspected, it was uncomfortably tight. Carrie inspected the situation for a moment before nodding. "Yes, this is workable. Here, hold the trousers up to your waist so I can see how short they are."

Without hesitation, he did what she asked, even though he felt a bit silly. She scrutinized the situation and then giggled again. "This should be a challenge. I knew you weren't as tall as Mr. Ashton, Jonathan, but I had no idea how short you are."

"Hey!" Jonathan shook his head. "Perhaps I'll decide to go to the concert after all."

Still laughing, Carrie gathered up the suit and put it back on the hanger. "Oh, you know I'm just teasing."

With slitted eyes, Jonathan glared at her from across the room, but it seemed he was well aware that Carrie was being silly.

"I'll just go work on making these alterations." Carrie smiled at each of them, making Robert's heart flutter, and then practically danced out of the room, leaving him staring after her.

"You might want to close your mouth before a fly lands on your tongue," Jonathan mused, pouring himself a cup of coffee from the carafe Robert had left on the table.

"My mouth was closed," Robert argued, though he wasn't quite sure that was actually true. He couldn't help it. Carrie was just a breath of fresh air. Everything about her made his breath catch and his heart hammer against his rib cage.

Taking a seat on the sofa, Jonathan sipped his coffee before asking, "What are your intentions exactly, if I may be so bold?"

Eyebrows arched at his boldness, Robert sank into his chair, folding his hands in front of him as he leaned forward on his knees. "Toward Carrie, I presume you're asking?"

Jonathan nodded slowly.

"She's lovely." The words came out easily this time. Perhaps he should've been trying to say that instead of "beautiful" like he had before. "I love spending time with her. Ever since we danced together at the Ashtons' wedding, I haven't been able to get her off my mind."

Again, Jonathan's head rocked back and forth–slowly. "But what are your intentions toward her? Carrie is a dear friend of mine, and I'd hate to see her get hurt–by anyone–in any way."

Swallowing hard, Robert considered what Jonathan was saying and why he might be saying it. Was Jonathan under the impression that Carrie had feelings for him? Could she have said something of the nature to him, or was this just another one of his keen observations?

"I'm interested in seeing where this may go," he admitted. It was easier to say the words to Jonathan than it would've been to Carrie. "This voyage seems to be about new beginnings for all of us, and I'd like to think it's a good sign that the two of us have become reacquainted under such circumstances." A hopefulness Robert hadn't felt in a long time continued to surface, bubbling up in his chest and causing a more genuine smile to grace his face than he had experienced in ages.

When Jonathan's head rocked back and forth this time, it was a bit quicker, as if he could see that Robert meant every word he'd spoken. "Very well then," he finally conceded. "If you truly care for her, I won't stand in your way. In fact, I'll continue to be helpful however I can be. But if you hurt her...." A shadow passed over his face, morphing his features into something sinister. Robert could hold his own with most men, but he wouldn't want to face off against Jonathan. "Just know that I'll rip you limb from limb."

All Robert could think to say was, "Fair enough."

15

Carrie practically floated around her room once she finished the adjustments to Jonathan's suit. It hadn't taken her as long as she thought it might, even with the rudimentary sewing kit she'd brought with her on this trip. If she'd been accompanying a lady such as Mrs. Ashton, whose gowns might require a higher level of attention, she would've brought something more substantial, but she'd figured the basic kit would be enough for anything one of her gowns might require should she get a snag or tear.

She'd never dreamed she'd be adjusting one of Jonathan's suits so that another gentleman could accompany her to her first concert.

The smile on her face simply wouldn't falter, no matter how many times Carrie warned herself she was getting ahead of the situation. "Just breathe," she told herself. But every time she thought of Robert, her lungs restricted, making it hard to do just that.

With the suit altered in a way she was quite sure would fit the bill, she rapped on the door between the two rooms. Jonathan answered, an amused expression on his face.

Carrie looked past him but didn't see Robert anywhere. Disappointment settled over her. "Is he here?"

"Just stepped out for a bit." The smirk didn't change. "Is it done?"

"I think so." She handed the suit over for him to inspect.

He nodded. "This should do nicely. I'll tell him to pick you up at seven."

"What about dinner?" Thoughts of the night they'd shared together the evening before came to mind. She desperately wanted to dine with him again.

Chuckling, Jonathan said, "Fine. I'll send for you at six."

With a satisfied smile, Carrie went into her bedroom to select a gown for her first concert date.

Later that evening, after another jovial dinner in Jonathan's quarters, Carrie and Robert strolled arm in arm toward the large room where the concert would be held. Carrie wasn't certain what the name of the room was aboard the *Lusitania*, but she'd heard it called a reception room or an events parlor on some of the other ships.

As they approached, she felt Robert's arm flex slightly. Looking up into his face, she could tell he was concerned. "Don't worry," she assured him. "If I am welcome considering my position, I'm sure you are, too."

"It's not that," Robert said, though she didn't quite believe him. "I'm afraid we'll run into trouble."

Understanding what he was getting at, Carrie scanned the crowd for any signs that Victor was also there. She didn't see him, though. "Let's find a spot near the back?" She assumed someone like Victor would want to be in the front row, should he show up.

Robert nodded. "Preferably near a door–just in case."

"That sounds like a good idea to me." Carrie took a seat in the back near an exit, and Robert sat next to her. Around them, the other passengers buzzed with excitement as they discussed how lovely the concert might be. Carrie wanted to pick up the easy conversation she'd shared with Robert over dinner, but the thrill of getting to see Gretchen Flynn in concert made her unable to form a coherent sentence.

Or maybe it was the presence of the handsome man next to her that left her unable to speak.

At any rate, the music began pretty quickly after they'd taken their seats, so there was really no opportunity to talk anyway. Carrie folded her hands in her lap, intertwining her fingers, and twisting them in excitement as Ms. Flynn took the stage.

A beautiful, clear soprano voice filled the room. Carrie gasped, unable to believe just how beautiful Gretchen's voice was. The redhead was petite, but her voice was huge. With the accompaniment of a five piece orchestra, she began to sing one of the more popular songs that Carrie was familiar with. Tears filled her eyes as she listened to the incredible sound.

After a few moments, she turned her head to look at Robert and saw that he was just as moved as she was. Despite herself, she reached over and slid her hand into his. His fingers wrapped around hers in a slight squeeze. A smile formed on her lips as she turned back toward the stage.

Gretchen sang three more songs, two ballads, and one up-tempo number, before a couple bustled in and took the seats a couple of rows ahead of Carrie and Robert. She might not have even noticed if they weren't incredibly noisy and rude to the other people sitting nearby. The woman giggled loudly, almost like she was inebriated. When the man leaned over and whispered something to her, she laughed again, and this time, so did he.

That was when Carrie realized who he was.

Her eyes shifted to Robert to see if he'd noticed, too. Of course, he had. With a scowl on his face, he looked back in the direction of the stage, but Carrie could tell he wasn't happy. Neither was she. Why did Victor always have to show up and ruin everything?

When the woman he was with began to whisper loudly, the woman directly in front of Carrie raised one finger to her lips and said, "Shhh!"

Victor and his date turned around, an irritated scowl on his face. He looked the woman in the eyes and began to give her what-for. But instead of chewing her out, he looked past her, and his expression shifted again. While still irritated, he now looked a bit surprised–and then amused.

"Damn," Robert muttered as Victor began to laugh. "He's probably drunk."

"Should we just leave?" Carrie asked in a low voice. She wanted to stay and enjoy the concert, but it would be easy for them to duck out the door next to them. "I bet we can hear from outside."

Solemnly, Robert nodded. He stood, and Carrie followed him out the door. They were careful to close it quietly. It was a little rude for them to leave in the middle of the concert, but the last thing Carrie wanted was to sit there and listen to Victor spew his hatred at them.

Outside on the deck, a few people were walking by, enjoying the evening air, but for the most part, it was secluded. Sound filtered through the door well enough that she could make out the words to the song Gretchen was singing, something about a man she once loved that she wanted to spend the rest of her life with, but now he was gone. It was a beautiful, melancholy song, and when she met Robert's eyes, Carrie knew in her heart that she felt the same way about him as the woman in the song.

His dark eyes caressed her face as he reached for her hand, pulling him over to her. Carrie placed her palm on his strong shoulder and leaned into him as his other arm came around her waist. In perfect time, they moved together to the rhythm of the song, which seemed to match the beat of the ocean far beneath their feet. Her gaze never wavered from his handsome face.

"You're so beautiful, Carrie," Robert murmured, his voice a deep whisper. "I feel like I've known you forever. Whenever we are together, nothing else in the world matters to me."

Her breath staggered as she fought to force out an exhale. "I feel the same way about you." A smile slipped into place as she inclined her head toward his. He moved in her direction, and there beneath a blanket of stars, Robert Crawford kissed her, sending Carrie's head spinning and her heart thrumming against her chest.

"Well, well, what do we have here? Lovebirds sucking face."

Victor's voice cut between them like a knife. Carrie took a step back, turning to face the millionaire who swayed on his feet as he approached them. She was sure it had nothing to do with the movement of the ship as the scent of whisky hit her nostrils.

"Mr. Anderson, we came out here to get away from you," Robert told him bluntly. "You've had too much to drink. You should go to bed."

"Go to bed?" The drunkard took a few more steps toward them. Carrie grabbed Robert's arm and stepped behind him. "Since when does a nobody like you tell me what to do? You're out here kissing my girl, and I'm gonna put an end to it."

"I'm not your girl." Carrie glared at him. "Go away and leave us alone."

"That's where you're wrong." He took another step forward but lost his balance and took a few steps back before catching it again. "If I say you're my girl, you're my girl. I'm Victor Anderson, goddammit."

"All right, Mr. Anderson. That's enough." Robert stepped toward him, clearly trying to help, but Victor didn't want his help. Instead, he swung a clumsy fist in Robert's direction, catching him in the lip.

Carrie squealed and covered her mouth with both hands. Hastily, she looked around for help.

It wasn't needed, though. As soon as Victor connected with the first punch, Robert clearly decided he wasn't going to be the man's punching bag anymore. He cocked back a right hook and let it fly, connecting with Victor's nose. Then, he threw a left jab and hit him in the eye.

Victor tipped backward and couldn't recover this time, landing on his bottom on the deck. Blood from his nose spurted between his fingers as he tried to cover it. "You bastard!" he shouted at Robert, trying to get up. "You're going to regret that! You just wait and see!"

Carrie had seen enough. Taking Robert by the arm, she pulled him away before Victor could manage to get off the ground. "Come on," she insisted. "Let's get away from him before he does something else."

At first, Robert wouldn't budge, his feet planted firmly on the deck, but after she yanked on him a few times, he reluctantly turned and went with her. Carrie rushed him along, not paying much attention to where they were going until they were far enough away that Victor couldn't easily catch up to them.

Robert must have realized they were lost. He said, "It's this way," and took her hand, pulling her down a hallway. Within a few minutes, they arrived back at their rooms. Carrie was glad he was good with directions because she would've been totally lost and had to find a steward.

She rushed him into her room to the bathroom where she wet a cloth and held it to his split lip. "What in the world is the matter with that man?" she murmured, pressing the washcloth to Robert's bloody mouth. "He's lost his mind."

"He's always been that way." It was difficult for Robert to talk while she was pressing against his mouth, but she understood him. "He's a rich prick who thinks he is better than everyone else." As soon as the sentence was out of his mouth, he apologized. "I shouldn't use language like that in front of a lady."

With a giggle, Carrie said, "I'm not exactly a lady."

"You are to me. You're the only lady that matters."

Swallowing the lump in her throat, Carrie lowered the bloody cloth away from his lip. The bleeding had stopped, but even if it hadn't, she didn't care. When Robert pressed his lips against hers again, she leaned into him, parting her lips and tasting him for the first time. His mouth was warm and soft, just like she'd always dreamed it would be.

After a moment, he pulled away from her. "I'm falling for you, Carrie Boxhall." He ran his thumb along her cheek. "Falling like a star from the heavens, and I don't care where I land or how bad it hurts."

With a smile, Carrie said, "I'll be your soft place to fall."

16

The next few days passed in a whirlwind as Carrie spent as much time as possible with Robert. Aboard *Lusitania*, it was as if they were in their own private world, their own secret bubble, and the outside world didn't matter. They could take their meals together, stroll around the deck holding hands, and sit in one another's company unchaperoned talking about life–their hopes and dreams–and anything and everything that mattered to them.

For the most part, Carrie had forgotten all about Victor Anderson. Though the thought of him sneaking up on them sometimes invaded her thoughts, she managed to put it out of her mind most of the time. He hadn't bothered them one bit since the concert. Robert had proven he was more than capable of protecting her and himself. Still, from time to time, she'd see a dark shadow pass over his face and wondered if he wasn't thinking about his old employer. While there were perks to being on the ship–such as a lack of responsibility and mundane tasks to attend to each day–it was also a bit of a disadvantage because they couldn't be completely rid of Mr. Anderson.

With the sun shining bright above them, Carrie and Robert strolled down the promenade, breathing in the fresh sea air and listening to the laughter of children playing nearby. It always made

Carrie smile to hear them. She missed Henry terribly. Letting out a sigh, she tried not to think of the Ashtons. They were her family, after all. If Mrs. Ashton went into labor before she got back, and she missed the birth, she'd be disappointed.

"Is something the matter?" Robert asked, stopping and pulling her over to the railing. Leaning his elbow on top of the barrier, he said, "You look distraught."

Carrie let out a low chuckle. "I'm sorry. No, everything is perfectly fine. I was just hoping Ms. Meg doesn't go into labor while I'm away. I'd love to be there for the birth of her baby."

He nodded in understanding. "Do you like children, Carrie?"

"I love them," she admitted, feeling her face flush. "Little Henry is so sweet. Lizzie and Ruth are a handful sometimes, but I do enjoy playing with their dolls and boats and things with them."

A grin brightened his face. "I think you'd be a wonderful mother someday, Carrie. It's clear you're very caring."

She had to look away, her eyes dropping to the tips of her shoes where they peeked out beneath her long blue gown. "Thank you. It will make it more difficult to travel the world." Another chuckle escaped her as she managed to lift her gaze to meet his. "I do love to go on adventures when I'm given the opportunity."

"Oh, I think lots of people are able to travel with their children. Look around us." He gestured at where the little ones were playing with a ball further down the deck. Carrie noted the smile on his face. It appeared to be genuine, as if he, too, liked children. "Perhaps you'll marry a rich gentleman who can hire a team of nannies for you."

The thought of marrying someone other than Robert made her smile falter a bit, but it was too soon for them to be speaking about anything of that nature, even in their *Lusitania* bubble. "Do you think my rich husband will allow me to take our brood of children on a safari trek to the Conga?" she asked in a teasing voice. "Or to see the native people of Australia in their natural habitat?"

Laughing, he leaned back against the railing so both elbows protruded over the edge. "I'm sure he will if he has the right number of nannies aboard his various modes of transportation."

They shared a chuckle as Carrie imagined herself on a much smaller boat snaking her way down a wild river populated with all kinds of dangerous animals and insects, surrounded by at least half a dozen children–all of them having Robert's eyes and her hair.

"Look, Miss Carrie!" a familiar voice shouted from a few feet further down the railing. "I believe I've spotted another dolphin!"

Carrie whirled around to see Hannah standing there, pointing out at the sea. She looked around and noticed Mrs. Smythe snoozing in a deck chair not too far away.

Walking over, Carrie took a spot next to Hannah with Robert behind her. "Well, Miss Hannah, I didn't even see you there."

"I've only just arrived, and look at the luck of it. See the dolphins? There's more than one this time."

Following where she was pointing, Carrie squinted a bit, but then she saw them–an entire pod of dolphins swimming alongside the ship. They weren't so far away that they couldn't easily be made out as they swam.

"Well, look at that!" Robert exclaimed, leaning down closer to Hannah. "Do you see that one has a baby alongside it?"

"Oh, it does!" she exclaimed, clapping her hands. "How wonderful!"

"It is remarkable," Carrie agreed, unable to pull her eyes away from the sight. "Hannah, I don't believe you've met my friend Mr. Crawford."

"How do you do?" Hannah didn't turn around to greet him, likely for fear of missing the excitement in front of her.

"It's a pleasure to meet you," Robert replied. Carrie stole a glance at him and couldn't help but grin at the way he was pointing out the dolphins to Hannah. He told her some amusing facts about the species, information Carrie didn't even know, about how fast they swim and how often they come up for air. Robert was an encyclopedia of information, and seeing him interact so well with Hannah solidified her thoughts that he would, one day, make a wonderful father.

After about ten minutes, the dolphins rambled off to some other part of the sea, fading from view. "Well, I suppose they've had enough excitement for one day," Carrie said with a sigh. "Maybe they don't enjoy staring up at our ship nearly as much as we like watching them."

"That's too bad." The young girl let out a deep breath. "I suppose I should get back to Mrs. Smythe now."

Carrie patted her on the shoulder. "I hope the rest of your day is pleasant."

"Thank you." The words seemed forced. Carrie knew Hannah wasn't all that fond of her governess.

"It was charming to meet you, Miss Hannah." Robert offered his hand.

A genuine smile lit Hannah's face as she shook his hand. "You as well, sir." Then, leaning closer to Carrie, she whispered, "This one is even more handsome than Mr. Lane."

Biting down on her lip to keep from laughing, Carrie whispered back, "He is very good looking." She looked up at Robert, and their eyes met. She knew he'd heard her, and she didn't mind one bit.

As Hannah headed off to meet her governess, Carrie slipped her arm through Robert's. "Now, that was an adventure. Do you suppose we'll see anything like that on our journey up the Congo?"

"Oh? Am I coming with you?" Robert teased. "Don't you think your husband and children might mind if I tag along?"

Feeling heat rush to her cheeks, Carrie went along with the joke. "Oh, I don't think he'll mind one bit. I intend to marry a generous man."

Robert leaned down so close that his breath tickled her neck, "Any man willing to share you with another is a fool."

Her breath caught in her throat as she turned her face toward him, their lips so close she could practically feel his mouth on hers. What would it hurt to share just a little kiss? Even out here in public?

The sound of heavy footsteps clomping toward them had both of their heads spinning around, the moment stolen away. "There he is!" Victor approached them, his arm extended, his finger pointing directly at Robert. "That's the man that assaulted me!"

"What?" The word left Carrie's lips as she pulled away to cover her mouth with both hands. How dare Victor make such an accusation against Robert. "That's not true!"

The man behind Victor was dressed in a uniform that declared he was part of the *Lusitania* staff, but something about him seemed to drip authority. As he stepped forward, Carrie realized this was the ship's constable, the man in charge of rounding up any ruffians or troublemakers.

"Mr. Anderson, you know that's not true," Robert began. "You struck me first."

"That's a bold face lie!" Victor's finger continued to wag in Robert's face.

"All right, all right," the constable said, stepping forward. "I'll handle this now, Mr. Anderson."

"Sir, I was there," Carrie began. "I saw the whole thing–"

"Yes, yes," he said dismissively. "I'm afraid I'm going to have to take Mr. Crawford here down for questioning." The constable, who'd had yet to name himself, pulled a pair of handcuffs from the pocket of his jacket.

"Handcuffs?" Robert's eyes nearly doubled in size. "That won't be necessary. I'm more than happy to come with you, Officer."

"That's Constable Pierce, thank you," he replied. Tall with dark hair and a handlebar mustache, the man had to be at least twenty years older than the rest of them and spoke with the authority of someone who was used to giving orders.

Sort of like Victor Anderson.

"Yes, Constable Pierce," Robert replied politely. "I can promise you I don't need to be restrained."

"Of course he does! Look at my face!" Victor pointed at his eye, which was still black and blue, the swelling having gone down so at least it opened all the way. His nose was also a bit swollen, though it didn't appear to be broken.

"My lip is still split, and I don't see anyone trying to put handcuffs on you," Robert pointed out.

"You accosted me first!" Victor shouted, leaning up on his tiptoes so he was almost Robert's height. "Don't you know who I am?"

"I should. I worked for you for three years," Robert calmly reminded him.

At those words, Constable Pierce hesitated a moment. "This is a former employee?"

"That's right." Victor no longer attempted to hide the truth behind the situation. "And he accosted me when I fired him."

Ignoring the crowd of people beginning to gather around them, Carrie said, "You didn't fire him. He quit because you wouldn't take no for an answer from me, Mr. Anderson."

Once again, recognition dawned on Constable Pierce's face. He blew out a breath. "Mr. Crawford, come with me to my office so I can get to the bottom of this. I've already taken a statement from Mr. Anderson."

"Yes, of course. I'll go peaceably," Robert said like the gentleman he was.

"And you, miss? What is your name?" The older gentleman inclined his head toward Carrie.

"Carrie Boxhall, sir."

"And are you a First Class passenger?"

"I am," she assured him, a bit embarrassed.

"And is Mr. Crawford staying with you in your rooms?" Constable Pierce's voice seemed to carry across the boat deck, leaving people gasping at the scandal.

"No, of course not. He's staying with a mutual friend, Jonathan Lane." Carrie felt her face turning bright red at the accusation.

"Oh, yes." The constable nodded as if he recognized Jonathan's name for some reason. But then, knowing her friend, Carrie surmised that Jonathan had already made the acquaintance of every important person on the ship, especially the one in charge of keeping law and order. "Very well. Come along, Mr. Crawford."

"I shall come, too," Mr. Anderson announced, his chin in the air.

"That won't be necessary." A stern look from the constable put Victor in his place. "I shall handle the situation from here."

"But–" Victor began, but he was cut off by the man who was truly in charge.

"I said I'll handle it."

Victor shrunk back a few steps. "Fine then."

Recognizing what was about to happen. Carrie squeezed Robert's arm and took off through the crowd before she found herself without Robert in Victor's presence. She knew she wouldn't be permitted to go along with the constable and him to the office, and the last thing she wanted was to be left alone with Victor—even amidst the crowd of people who'd come to see what was happening.

She slipped through the bystanders as quickly as she could and made her way inside, practically running back to her room. She needed to reach safety before Victor found her.

And she needed to find Jonathan.

17

"He's a real piece of work, this fellow," Victor said once Robert had reached Constable Pierce's office. "A real animal! Struck me in the face for no reason whatsoever the other night. I've been looking everywhere for him ever since, but he's been doing his best to stay away from me. Shacking up with that woman of ill-repute, no doubt."

It was the last part that had Robert wanting to turn around and punch Victor again. He'd listened to the man bash him all the way to the office, but saying something ugly about Carrie was a good way to earn himself another black eye.

"I thought you said she was your girl." Constable Pierce hovered above the chair he was about to sit down in behind a desk in the small office that occupied nearly one-half of the entire space.

"She... was." Victor couldn't keep all of his lies straight, it seemed. "I mean, she wanted to be. But I rejected her."

"So she took up with Mr. Crawford here, and then he just attacked you out of nowhere?" Constable Pierce frowned at Victor, clearly having figured out exactly what sort of man the millionaire really was. "All right then. As I said before, there's no reason for you to be here, sir. I've already gotten your statement. I'll take Mr. Crawford's and then–"

"And then what?" Victor interrupted, clearly agitated. "You'll just let him go?"

"If that's what I see fit." Constable Pierce might've been older, but he wasn't weak or cowardly. He folded his arms across his chest and stared at the man in the doorway.

Victor grumbled. "Fine. But you should know, if you handle this poorly, I'll make sure the authorities know about it as soon as we disembark. I'm an important fellow, I'll remind you."

"Yes, yes. I understand. Now, go on about your business, Mr. Anderson." With that, Constable Pierce crossed the room, ushered the complainant out, and then closed the door. He let out a loud sigh on his way back to his desk. "You used to work for him?"

"For almost four years." It was hard for Robert to admit he'd stuck around for that long.

"Well, I'm not sure how anyone could do that," the constable muttered as he took his seat. "Go ahead and tell me what's going on, Crawford. And make it snappy. I've got other business to attend to."

Nodding, Robert said, "It's pretty simple. I met Miss Boxhall several years ago. We've seen each other at events from time to time as we both work for wealthy families. I had no idea she was going to be here, but on the day we left, I spotted her talking to Mr. Anderson. It was clear she was uncomfortable. He is a bit of a womanizer, and as I think you can tell, he doesn't like to take no for an answer."

"I've seen that first hand," he muttered. "Go on."

"The next day, I saw him talking to her again, really harassing her this time, and I ended up getting into it with him then. Nothing physical, but I quit my job over it. I've been sleeping on the couch in Jonathan Lane's room since."

"Oh, yes." He nodded in recognition of the name. "And how are the pair of you acquainted?"

"Both Mr. Lane and Miss Boxhall work for the Ashtons. They are traveling together on a personal matter for Mrs. Ashton."

"I understand. What happened the night of the concert?" The man was certainly getting to the point now.

"Miss Boxhall and I went together. Even though I'm not technically a First Class passenger, Mr. Lane gave up his seat for me to be able to attend. Part way through the performance, Mr. Anderson walked in with some woman I didn't recognize. They were being obnoxiously loud, and I thought they might be drunk. Miss Boxhall and I didn't want any part of that, so we stepped outside to enjoy the music from there. Mr. Anderson must've gotten jealous because he came outside–alone–and started accosting us. He threw the first punch and I... ended it." Robert shrugged that was the gist of it, more or less.

Constable Pierce took a deep breath and then nodded. "You say he punched you first?"

"Yes. In the lip." He lifted his hand to indicate where the mark could still be seen.

"Did anyone witness this?"

"Only Miss Boxhall, as far as I know," Robert admitted. "Listen, sir, I know that Mr. Anderson is wealthier and more influential than I, but I'm not a troublemaker. I wouldn't have any reason to punch my former employer unless he was attacking me or making trouble for Miss Boxhall or another woman."

Again, Pierce's head rocked back and forth. "Yes, that makes sense. Listen, Mr. Crawford, this is a relatively small ship compared to, say, a large city like New York or Liverpool. What you and Mr. Anderson do once you disembark is not my concern, but while you're here, do your best to stay away from one another. It's not in the best interest of anyone aboard for the pair of you to be at each other's throats."

"I understand, sir." The last thing Robert wanted was to have another altercation with Victor–or anyone, for that matter.

"Very well then. For now, I'll leave you both be. Just don't let anything else like this happen again, Crawford. You may go." Constable Pierce picked up a pen and scribbled a few notes on a pad, which Robert assumed were notes for himself in case Victor didn't let this be the end of it. Without having to be told twice, he thanked the constable and got up to make his way back to Jonathan's room.

He didn't make it much farther than one of the hallways leading to First Class accommodations when Victor appeared almost out of nowhere. He certainly was good at that. "What are you doing here?" he snarled.

"I'm going to my room. Listen, Mr. Anderson, Constable Pierce said we should just stay away from one another, and I wholeheartedly agree. There's no reason for us to cause trouble and annoy all of the other passengers." Even as Robert spoke, a few of their fellow passengers skirted around them in the narrow hallway.

Victor's eyes narrowed. "I know what you think you're doing. You think if you can manage to last this entire trip that when you get back to dry land you can find other work. Well, I've got news for you." He jabbed Robert in the shoulder with a finger. "I'm Victor Anderson. My family is the wealthiest, most influential in all of New York City—in all of the world. And I will ruin you. I'll make certain that you don't work another day in your life for anyone!"

While it was tempting to push Victor away from him, Robert simply stepped around him, ignoring his threats. "You don't scare me," he said over his shoulder.

"Well, I should scare you!" Victor shouted after him. "I mean it when I say you're finished, Robert Crawford! Finished!"

Robert managed to slide between a few families and other passengers walking down the hall so that it would be difficult for Victor to catch him. When Jonathan's room came into view up ahead, he let out a deep breath and rushed to knock on the door.

Before he reached it, he felt a strong hand clamp down on his shoulder and might've whirled around to throw a punch if he hadn't heard Jonathan's voice. "I was just looking for you. Is everything all right?"

"Yes, yes." Robert reached up to drag his hand down his face, thankful it wasn't Victor. "It's been a day."

He patted Robert's back a few times and then stepped over to open the door. "I can imagine. Let's have a drink. Victor had Pierce take you in for the fight the other night?"

Inside of the room, Jonathan stepped over to a decanter and poured them both a brandy. Robert accepted and drank it down before answering. "He did. He's such an arrogant bastard." He walked to the glass door where he had a better view of the ocean, which seemed to help calm him.

"I must've made it to Pierce's office just as you were leaving. I had a few words with him. Seems the matter is settled so long as nothing else happens between the two of you." Jonathan joined him, taking a drink from his glass.

"That's good to know." Robert's eyes didn't lift from the vast blue expanse in front of them. "He threatened to ruin me."

Again, Jonathan's hand was a comfort as he clapped his shoulder. "You don't need to worry about that. A man like Victor Anderson isn't used to having anyone stand up to him. You've done that several times now. He's still trying to push you around because he thinks he can. It's a shame, really. With all that money, he could do some good in this world. Instead, he'd rather use it to live fast and loud and do whatever the hell tickles his fancy at the moment."

Robert let that soak in a bit. It was true. If he was ever in a position to have enough money to do as he pleased, he would certainly use some of those funds to help others. "The Ashtons are known for their charity work. Was Mr. Ashton always like that? Giving and generous? Or was that Mrs. Ashton's doing?" Robert wasn't sure why he asked the question, but he knew that Charles and Victor had a similar upbringing. Both of them had been born with silver spoons in their mouths. Was Charles just a better man than Victor? Or was it something more?

A crooked smirk formed on Jonathan's face. "Oh, Charlie's had his moments. But even before he met his wife, he was a giving man. The pair of them were betrothed when they were small children. He had a few years when he ran wild, but in the end, he always knew he was going to be with Mrs. Ashton."

An eyebrow raised as Robert took that all in. He'd heard bits and pieces, but it was interesting to have it all explained to him. He returned his gaze to the ocean. It was almost dinner time, and the sun was beginning to paint the sky with pinks and yellows. "Well, I certainly feel quite honored to have met both of you. Knowing that Mr. Ashton is willing to take me on in some capacity makes all the trouble worth it." He thought of Carrie and how lucky he was to have been reunited with her. "I'm a lucky fellow to have come across you."

Behind him, Robert thought he heard the creak of a door and turned, hoping to see Carrie standing there. She had to be worried. He needed to tell her he was back and everything was well.

But when he turned around, she wasn't there. He must've heard something else.

"We will be lucky to have you, I'm sure," Jonathan said, though he suddenly seemed distracted. "I told Carrie to go lie down. Her head was hurting. I'm going to go check on her."

As much as Robert would've liked to be the one to make sure she was well, it wasn't his place. He thanked Jonathan again as he headed through the door between their rooms and then fixed his eyes on the ocean. Hopefully, this was the end of his trouble with Victor Anderson and the beginnings of a new life for him—with Carrie.

18

Carrie sank down onto a chair that looked out over the water. The breeze on the deck helped the pain in her head, but nothing could help the ache in her heart.

All of this was because of the Ashtons. She should've known better. Robert was a kind man, but even he could be persuaded to act unscrupulous when it came to making his way in this world. Not that his idea for motorcoaches wasn't wonderful. She was certain Mr. Ashton would agree and use it to benefit his business as well, but it was nice to think that Robert was interested in her because he had true feelings for her, not because he needed a job.

Sniffling, she wiped her nose in the handkerchief she kept with her all the time and tried not to cry. A thousand dreams of a life with Robert shattered, the image dropping like shards of glass in her mind's eye. Whatever had she been thinking?

"Carrie, how are you feeling?" Jonathan's voice dripped with concern as he stepped out and sat in the chair next to hers. "I thought I heard you come into my room."

Dabbing at her eyes with the handkerchief, Carrie stayed turned away from her friend for a moment, trying not to cry in front of him. "I'm fine."

"You don't seem fine," he noted. "Carrie, if you overheard what we were talking about–"

"I feel so foolish!" she blurted, interrupting him. "I thought he was actually interested in me. This whole time, he's just been using me to get to Mr. Ashton." She shook her head, willing the tears not to fall from her cheeks.

A soft chuckle from Jonathan had her spinning in her chair. He was shaking his head. "Oh, dear."

"It's not funny. You certainly didn't think it was funny that time you thought Edward was whispering sweet-nothings in that other man's ear at the Christmas party."

All amusement drained from Jonathan's face. "That's true. I didn't think it was funny. But I was wrong–and so are you." Standing, he took a few steps toward the door. "I'm not going to get in the middle of this, Carrie, but you do need to speak to Robert. I know you well enough to understand this is just you doubting yourself, thinking you don't measure up. Well, I know you do. And so does he."

Carrie's mouth dropped open, and she tried to form another argument, but no words came to her lips, and then Jonathan disappeared inside.

Taking a shaky breath, Carrie stood and paced to the railing, looking out over the ocean. No matter how turbulent she felt on the inside, the water always seemed to soothe her. She knew that not everyone felt that way. Jonathan certainly didn't feel calm when he looked out at the wide expanse. Mr. Ashton almost couldn't do it at all. Would her opinion change if she ever found herself submersed with nothing but miles of blue liquid all around her? Probably so.

"Eighteen minutes…." The warning slipped from her lips as she pictured Ruth's face as she told her that she wouldn't have nearly as much time to get off *Lusitania* as the passengers aboard *Titanic* had had.

"What's that?"

Robert's voice startled her. Carrie jumped a little and pulled herself from her thoughts, turning to face him. She had no idea what, if anything, Jonathan had told him, other than the fact that he needed to come and speak to her, but he stood there with a concerned look on his handsome face, nothing but caring pooled in those chocolate eyes.

"Oh, nothing." She shook her head, leaving all thoughts of Ruth and her silly game behind. "I was just... thinking about something Mrs. Ashton's niece said. How did it go with Pierce?" Why was she asking that when what she really wanted to know was if he was interested in her or just in need of employment?

He nodded and gestured for the chairs. She didn't want to move from the railing, but she joined him anyway. "He questioned me for a few moments and then let me go. The constable suggested Victor and I stay away from one another. I saw him on my way back here and told him as much, but I'll be shocked if he listens."

Her head rocked back and forth as she considered his words, but she wasn't really listening. While she was concerned about the situation with Victor, it wasn't at the top of her priorities. Just being near him made her heart race and her mind fill with thoughts of what they could have together one day.

But now, with all of these concerns brought to light, all she could think about was whether or not she'd acted impulsively.

"Carrie, it's obvious something is bothering you." He reached for her, but instinctively, she leaned away. The look of heartbreak on his face tugged at her heartstrings, but she couldn't help feeling the way she did. "I understand it must've been embarrassing for you, having all those people stare at us while Victor accused me of picking a fight with him."

"It's not that," she said quickly. She watched as confusion settled in on his handsome face. "I knew you were in the right and had no problem telling anyone who was listening that that was the case."

"Then what is it?"

His confusion softened her a bit. "I just think maybe we're not both in this for the same reason. This... relationship. Whatever it is."

He stared at her for a moment, and she half expected him to say she was right, that he wasn't in it for her, that he simply wanted to work for Mr. Ashton. But when he spoke, his words sounded like home. "I'm in it for you, Carrie. I know we haven't spent a tremendous amount of time together, yet, but every moment I spend with you is delightful and whispers of promises of a lovely life for years to come."

Tears brimmed in her eyes again, but even hearing him say such beautiful words didn't alleviate the doubts that had crept in when she'd heard him thank Jonathan for getting him a job, talking about how lucky he was to have ran into him here. "I think… I need some time to think about all of this, Robert. It's all happened so fast."

"I understand." She could hear the disappointment in every word Robert spoke. "Take your time, Carrie. I'm so sorry I've offended you. That's the last thing in the world I would ever want to do."

"No, it's fine." She could hear the sadness in her tone and knew it was a lie. It registered with him as well. The truth of the matter was, no matter how badly she wanted to just sweep it under the rug, what she'd heard him say when he thought she wasn't listening hurt her to her core.

Robert lifted a hand and reached toward her, as if he might pat her on the shoulder, but then, thinking better of it, he dropped his hand to his side. "Whenever you're ready to speak to me, I'll be ready to listen, Carrie. You mean so much to me. I hope you know that."

She found herself nodding but didn't bother to open her mouth. If any words came tumbling between her lips at this point, they'd all sound wrong.

He gave her a weak smile, and then, without another word, slipped back through the door that separated her quarters from Jonathan's.

There was no use trying to stop the tears from falling now. Carrie turned back toward the ocean and let them slip from her eyes, trailing down her cheeks and dripping from her chin into the vast abyss.

Had she really dreamed the whole situation? Was Robert really only in this for the money? It seemed foolish for her to think that he would go to such trouble to spend time with her when she already had Jonathan's promise of an introduction to Mr. Ashton, but he wouldn't be the first suitor to disappoint her. One by one, the faces of the other men she'd felt a connection to marched by in her mind's eye, each of them more disappointing than the last.

There had been a time when she thought she might not marry at all. She'd resolved herself to living vicariously through Mr. and Mrs. Ashton and their happy family. While she'd never imagined she'd end up an old maid, her chances of meeting someone at her age were slim, especially since she spent most of her time in service to the Ashtons. From the moment she'd agreed to come on this trip, she'd been hoping she might meet someone. It wasn't her only reason for saying yes, of course. She wanted the adventure and to do something to help her wonderful mistress, but at the end of the day, she'd be lying if she said she hadn't had a bit of hope that maybe she'd be swept off her feet by some dashing young man.

And she had been. Not by just any gentleman but by the man she'd been pining over for years. Now, here they were with him in the other room contemplating his life choices and her crying salty tears into the ocean.

The moment she heard Jonathan step through the door, she started wiping at her cheeks, not wanting him to see her cry. He had to have known they hadn't worked it out. He would've spoken to Robert. "Carrie?" His voice was soothing as he stood next to her. "What would you like to do for dinner? You don't want to go back into the dining hall, do you?"

Immediately, she shook her head. "No, I think I'd rather eat in my room. Alone."

"Would you like for me to join you? I don't mind."

"No, that's okay." Carrie knew he was just being polite. Jonathan enjoyed spending time with the other First Class passengers. For so many years, he'd been stuck with the other servants in the background. This voyage was his opportunity to shine as well, and she wouldn't be the one to take that away from him.

"All right then. I'll arrange for it. But Carrie, please don't be upset. You have to know Robert truly does care for you. I know he'll prove it to you." Jonathan reached over and touched her shoulder.

"I hope so." She turned to face him, fighting a quiver in her bottom lip. "We'll be at Liverpool soon, though, and we'll have business to attend to. We'll all be on our way back to New York, and then, well, he'll have a new life to start, with Mr. Ashton's help."

Jonathan nodded. "I think that's the plan, but I'm certain that every dream he has for his future contains you in a starring role, Carrie."

She nodded. "I hope so. Time will tell."

"Try to get some rest. It's been a rough day." Jonathan gave her another sympathetic smile and then headed out.

Carrie's stomach rumbled, but she wasn't hungry. She'd pick at whatever was brought to her for dinner, but she couldn't imagine eating much, not the way she was feeling.

Every dream she had of her future recently had contained Robert as well. Now, those images began to twist and turn into a nightmare where he was nowhere to be found and she was back in New York utterly alone.

19

Later that evening, Robert sat in Jonathan's quarters alone eating a meager dinner. He appreciated the trouble his host kept going to in order to ensure he could eat in his room unbothered. Not only did it allow him to avoid Victor, it gave him time to think.

From the room on the other side of the thin wood door that separated the chambers, occasionally, he heard the clank of silverware on china and knew that Carrie was sitting over there eating her dinner alone as well. It broke his heart a little to think about it. If it were up to him, the two of them would be together.

Letting out a sigh, he wiped his mouth on a napkin and pushed back from the table, finished despite having only eaten about half of what was on the plate. It had always been difficult for him to eat when he was upset, and at the moment, all he could think about was the misunderstanding with Carrie.

She'd heard him correctly, of course. He had said that he was thankful to have met Jonathan so that he could meet Mr. Ashton, and he meant every word of it. That didn't take away from the fact that he was also quite pleased to have become reacquainted with Miss Boxhall herself. In fact, that would be the highlight of this voyage—and quite possibly the highlight of his life.

He'd been spending a lot of time thinking about Carrie ever since that first day when he'd run into her talking to Victor on the deck. He wished he would've realized then that Carrie was in distress. How many times had he avoided helping a woman because the lady in question was being too polite? He couldn't go back and help any of the women Victor Anderson had taken advantage of in the past, but he vowed he'd never let another woman become a victim of the womanizer, no matter what.

He heard a sigh from the other room and then what sounded like Carrie also pushing her food away. It brought a smile to his lips, despite the circumstances. He could picture her over there, her beautiful mouth drawn into a tight line as she contemplated what to do. Hope had not left him. He was fairly certain she'd come back around after she had some time to consider the situation. She did care for him, after all. And he knew he'd never be able to walk away from her, no matter the misunderstanding.

The door to the room opened with a slight squeak, and for a moment, he hoped it was Carrie coming over from the adjoining suite. He tried not to show his disappointment when Jonathan walked in. The fragrance of roasted duck lingered on him as he flashed Robert a kind smile. "Dinner must've been good," Robert joked.

"The duck sauce was to die for." Jonathan chuckled and joined him in the sitting area. "How was your meal?" His eyes went to the half-eaten portion still on Robert's plate. "Not that good, I'm guessing."

Letting out a chuckle, Robert said, "Well, I suppose it's hard to eat with a bit of a broken heart."

Jonathan's smile became more empathetic. "No need for that. I've known Carrie for a long time, and I'm certain she'll come around. She just needs to get her thoughts together. She's not the most confident person in the world, I'm afraid."

Robert had figured that much out, but it didn't stop him from saying, "Well, she should be. A woman of her beauty, her kindness and intelligence?" He shook his head. "Any man would be lucky to have her and a fool for not realizing what he had."

"Very true, but then, in my experience there are more foolish men in this world than wise ones. She's had her heart broken a few times, unfortunately."

Robert let that settle. He'd never want to be the one to make Carrie cry. He hoped Jonathan was right when he said she just needed some time. That was his gut feeling as well. But time wasn't something they had a lot of, at least, not aboard the *Lusitania*. Before too much longer, they'd be docking in Liverpool. Carrie and Jonathan would go on about their business in Southampton, and Robert would find his way back to New York City. After all, his only business in Britain was for a man he no longer worked for, so there was no reason for him to stay, not unless he could be of service to his new friends in some way. Since neither of them had asked him to join them on the rest of their trip, he planned to head back to New York, gather his meager belongings from his room at Mr. Anderson's place, and find a room to board in until his circumstances bettered.

After that, well, he had some ideas about that, but at the moment, with Carrie upset at him, he thought it best to keep those ideas to himself.

"It's a lovely evening. Would you care to go for a stroll around the deck? I can guarantee that Victor is in the smoking lounge–at least for the moment. Wiley bugger never seems to stay in any one place too long." Jonathan shook his head. It was clear he was just as irritated at the millionaire as Robert was.

"Certainly. I'd like to get some fresh air." Robert stood and began to clear the dishes out of habit.

With a chuckle, Jonathan reminded him, "I'll call someone to take care of that. You've got to start living like a First Class passenger."

Shaking his head, Robert said, "I'm not sure I'd ever get used to people waiting on me."

"You will one day, when you're rich–a famous inventor."

Robert liked the sound of that–the inventor part. He had no need for all of the money people like Mr. Anderson kept stored up in their banks. If he had that sort of money, he'd be sure to use it to help people. "We'll see about that." The two of them shared a chuckle and headed out to the deck. Again, Robert wished Carrie was by his side, but she'd probably be happier in her room this night.

Out beneath the stars, several other people took in the cool breeze. The sound of soft music rolled across the breeze from somewhere inside the ship. It sounded like the musicians who'd accompanied Gretchen the other night entertaining First Class passengers. He paused for a moment, thinking of the dance he'd shared with Carrie, before hurrying on to catch up to Jonathan who walked fast for a man taking a stroll. That seemed to be his nature, always on the go.

"It's a beautiful night," Jonathan murmured. He had no problem looking up at the sky, but whenever his gaze shifted so that he was looking out at the body of water around them, Robert could see the hesitation.

"You don't like to talk about it, do you?" He hoped his tone was friendly enough that Jonathan wouldn't feel obligated to discuss *Titanic* now—or offended.

Shaking his head, Jonathan said, "No, not really. Most of us don't."

"I can't imagine what that must've been like." The two of them leaned against the railing for a moment as Jonathan took a few slow, deep breaths.

"It was utter hell," he finally said. "The only thing worse than watching that ship go down was the aftermath of it all." He bit his bottom lip for a second, an expression Robert had never seen from the confident man. "All the screaming. The crying from the people in the boats. The not knowing."

"Were you with Mrs. Ashton?" Again, Robert hoped he wasn't prying.

"No, I was with Mrs. O'Connell and her youngest daughter," he explained. "Charlie had gone back to find Meg, Ruth, and Mr. O'Connell. He insisted I get on the boat with Kelly. That was the hardest decision of my life. Once she was on the boat with her baby, and safe, it would've been easy for me to duck out and go find Charlie."

With a solemn nod, Robert asked, "Why didn't you?"

Watching him swallow a lump in his throat, Robert gave the other man a moment. Finally, Jonathan said, "Because the chances of all three of us men getting home safely were slim. I had a feeling, if I got on the lifeboat, and Charlie managed to get Daniel—who had a cast on his arm at the time—on a lifeboat with Ruth and Meg, then Charlie's chances of surviving were greater than if I were with him. That's just how he is—always worried about someone else."

Nodding, Robert thought about what he would've done in a similar situation and prayed he'd never find out. "You made the right choice," he finally said. "I'm sure it meant a lot to Mrs. O'Connell to have you there."

"It did," Jonathan said. "But if Charlie would've stayed dead, I probably would've never forgiven myself."

"Stayed dead?" Robert asked, confused.

Turning to look at him, he said, "Yes. That's right. He died, but he came back to life."

"However did that happen?" Robert had never heard of such a thing.

"Mrs. Ashton's love brought him back." Jonathan spoke as if it were obvious, as if it should've been clear to anyone that love could do such a thing.

Shocked at the explanation, Robert needed a moment before he could respond. But just then, the two of them heard a commotion behind them and turned around. It sounded like a woman's voice. Shrill, and full of intensity, she said something that sounded like, "I told you no. I'm a married woman!"

Exchanging glances with Jonathan, Robert moved quickly to the dark shadow around a corner where the voice seemed to be coming from. He paused when he saw a familiar form lurking in the darkness, hovering over a much smaller shape of a woman.

"Come on, baby. Your husband isn't on board. What he doesn't know can't hurt him."

Victor's voice cut through Robert's eardrums like a shard of glass dragging over a chalkboard. His fists automatically clenched at his sides.

"Leave me alone. I don't care who you are!" The girl tried to pull away, but Victor had her by the arm. He began to laugh as she desperately tried to put some distance between them.

That was enough for Robert. He looked at Jonathan who gave him a nod, which assured Robert he'd be there if he needed him, but this fight was his.

"I think the lady said no." It wasn't the first time Robert had made such a statement to Victor, but he hoped it would be the last. As his former employer turned to face him, Robert cocked back his fist and rammed it into the nose he'd nearly broken only a few days earlier. The woman screamed as blood squirted everywhere.

"What the hell!" Victor shouted, reaching for his newly shattered face. "You ass—"

Before he could finish the insult, Robert punched him again. He connected with his cheek, then his jaw, and finally punched him in the stomach hard enough to send him doubling over. "Go ahead and try contacting Constable Pierce," Robert spat at him. "I don't give a rat's ass if I'm arrested for the rest of the trip. This is your final warning that when a woman doesn't want your advances, you need to back the hell off!"

With all of the noise drawing in a crowd, Victor backed away, his arm around his stomach. "You're going to regret this!" he shouted.

Robert stared after him as he slunk away into the night. Then, he turned to the woman. The petite redhead threw her arms around him, crying. "Thank you. Thank you so much!"

"What in the world is going on?"

Constable Pierce's voice was recognizable to Robert, and even though the poor woman was still sobbing against his chest, assuring him he'd done the right thing, dread filled the pit of his stomach.

"Victor Anderson was assaulting this woman," Jonathan explained to the constable. "We happened upon it. But he's gone off now."

The constable bent down to look at the deck where a few drops of blood were spattered. He shook his head. "Didn't I tell the two of you to leave one another alone?"

Before Robert could answer, the woman said, "This man saved me, sir. That horrible Mr. Anderson wanted his way with me and wouldn't take no for an answer. If it hadn't been for this man, well, I don't know what I would've done."

"Beg your pardon, Mrs. Hildegard." Constable Pierce bowed his head politely.

"Hildegard?" Robert repeated. The Hildegards were one of the richest families in all of New York. He'd had no idea who she was, and it didn't matter, so long as she needed help.

"Come by in the morning, Mr. Crawford." Constable Pierce sounded a bit exasperated. "I'll take your statement. Again."

"Yes, sir," he answered as Jonathan offered to walk Mrs. Hildegard to her room. Robert took a deep breath and shook out his aching hand. It seemed that Victor Anderson was going to be the death of him.

20

Silverware clanked on dishes as the large cafeteria-style room buzzed with conversation around them. When Carrie had asked Robert to join her there for breakfast, he'd been a bit reluctant. She assumed he was afraid they'd run into Victor, but she doubted someone like Mr. Anderson would ever take his breakfast in a room where there was an equal amount of Second Class passengers as there were people of his own social standing.

Robert was quiet as he sipped his coffee and took a few bites of his eggs. His eyes continued to dart around the room from time to time. Carrie considered eating faster so that they could leave, but she'd brought him here to apologize. It was just difficult to get the words out when he wasn't saying much of anything at all.

"I've thought about our discussion," she began, setting her fork down for a moment. "I want to apologize to you."

Robert's full attention was on her now. "Apologize? For what?"

"For how I behaved." It was nothing unusual for her face to heat when she was looking into Robert's eyes, but it was usually because he made her feel euphoric—not embarrassed. "I should've never thought that you would treat me so crassly, and I apologize for jumping to conclusions."

"You don't need to apologize," Robert said, practically in a whisper.

"I do, though," she disagreed. "I should've known better. Just because you're happy to have the opportunity to meet Mr. Ashton, that doesn't mean you're not equally grateful to have become reacquainted with me."

"I'm not equally grateful," Robert said plainly. Her stomach twisted into a knot. He must've had a chance to think about it and realize that meeting her was not that much of an opportunity after all.

"I understand," Carrie murmured.

"I don't think you do." Robert's large hand came down on hers for a moment with a light squeeze before he pulled it away. "If I never had the opportunity to meet Mr. Ashton or pitch my idea to any man of means, I'd still be overly joyful at our chance to reconnect, Carrie. You are far more important to me than anything else."

A small chuckle left her throat. "But… you have a chance to make your fortune."

"You are worth much more than money could ever buy, Carrie. And if I've given you the impression that I feel any differently, I apologize. I'm the one who should be saying he's sorry to you for ever making you feel like you were less important to me than money." The sincerity in his brown eyes cut through to her very soul.

Shaking her head, Carrie said, "You haven't. Only in a moment of misunderstanding, and that's mostly my fault. I have a tendency to jump to conclusions." Taking a deep breath, she continued, revealing more about herself than she ever liked to articulate. "I don't have a lot of faith in myself most of the time, I'm afraid."

"Well, you should," he said. "You're an amazing woman. Anyone who can't see that is a fool."

Feeling a weight lifted off her shoulders, Carrie thanked him, beaming a smile, and the two of them went back to eating their breakfast, talking about much less weighty topics. "We'll be in Liverpool before too long. Then what are your plans?" she asked him as they finished up.

"I'm not sure," he admitted. "I was thinking I might just turn around and go back to New York."

"That's probably for the best." It wasn't that Carrie didn't want to spend more time with him, but the more they were together, the harder it was for her to control her emotions. "We can meet once I'm back in New York and sort things out then."

With their breakfast gone, they stood, Robert pushing her chair in for her, and made their way out to the deck. "It is a lovely day," Robert noted, holding the door open for her. "We should be near the coast of Ireland in a few hours."

"That'll be lovely." Carrie stepped outside and felt the ocean air on her face for one of the last times. She was sad to know the voyage was almost over, but then, she'd have another adventure on the way home, she assumed. It would be nice to book a room near Robert's and not have him be forced to sleep on the sofa. "Would you care to go for a stroll?"

"Actually, I have to go speak to Constable Pierce again." Robert made a face as they stopped near the railing. "Victor put his hands on a woman last night, and I stopped him."

Carrie's eyes widened. "I had no idea."

He lowered his eyes. "I didn't want to worry you. But I'm sure Constable Pierce will handle it."

Her mouth dropped open as she struggled to find something to say. That awful Victor Anderson! She hoped Robert had knocked his block off.

Behind her, Carrie heard the familiar sound of Hannah's voice, and a smile lit her face. She turned to see the young girl pointing out into the water and excitedly calling to her governess who wasn't paying her any mind at all. At least she'd have someone to spend the day with.

"I'll catch up with you as soon as I've finished giving my statement—again," Robert told her.

"All right." Before he stepped away, Carrie reached out and put a hand on his arm, Ruth's words echoing through her mind. "Do be careful, Robert. You know what the rumors are, about what may happen once we get close to land."

His brow furrowed as his dark eyes met her lighter ones. "I'm not too concerned about it, Carrie. That being said, if anything should happen, please take care of yourself. I shouldn't want to have to wonder if you were on the ship looking for me when you should be safely tucked away in a lifeboat."

Carrie's breath caught in her throat. She remembered the few times Mr. Ashton had spoken about what happened on *Titanic*. He was always very clear that he was able to take care of himself and survive because he knew that everyone else he cared about was already on a lifeboat–including Jonathon.

"I will take care of myself," she promised.

With a nod, Robert leaned down and pressed his lips to hers. Carrie leaned up on her tiptoes to kiss him back, not caring that others may think it inappropriate. If it hadn't been for Ruth's voice playing over and over again in her mind, she might've been more demure, but her soul was stirred.

After a moment, Robert pulled away. "See you soon," he told her. She nodded and watched him walk away, praying it was true and they'd be back together in time for dinner.

The sound of Jonathan's footsteps approaching had her turning her head away from the spot where Robert had disappeared. "Where's Robert off to?" He stopped beside her, his hands pushed down into the pockets of his trousers.

"To speak to Constable Pierce," she replied. "But then, I suppose you already knew that."

Jonathan gave her a small smile and a shrug. "Possibly. It looks like someone may have spotted some more dolphins." Rather than tell her what he knew, he changed the subject, and she didn't blame him.

"We should go spend some time with her. We'll all be disembarking soon, and I will miss our new friend." Carrie began to walk toward Hannah, Jonathan walking along beside her.

"It's probably not a bad idea to keep an eye out," he muttered, scanning the horizon.

"Do you think we are in danger?" Carrie smiled and nodded politely at a couple passing by, but on the inside, she felt her heart begin to race.

"There's always some risk out here." He sounded nonchalant. "Even when there shouldn't be."

"Yes, I know that's true." She didn't think there was much risk of them hitting an iceberg at their current location, or for a piece of land to suddenly jut up out of the ocean and run them aground. She was more concerned about nefarious acts—like Germans performing an act of war.

"I'm sure we'll be fine." Jonathan's tone was not convincing, but Carrie did her best to put her worries aside as they took up a spot next to Hannah against the railing.

"Did you see another dolphin?" Jonathan asked, smiling at the girl.

"I think so!" She laughed, pointing out at the ocean. "Something leaped out of the water out there. It was gray. It had to be a dolphin."

Carrie caught Jonathan's eye, and they both smiled and shrugged. Sometimes, one's eyes played tricks on them when trying to decipher shadow from submerged mammal.

"Let's keep looking and see if any more leap out of the water," Jonathan suggested.

For the next hour or so, they searched for dolphins and chatted with other passengers who stopped whenever Hannah insisted she saw one. Mrs. Smythe gave Hannah permission to go along with them as they walked to other parts of the ship, Hannah keeping an eye out for dolphins while Jonathan and Carrie watched for... something else.

Around lunchtime, Carrie's stomach began to rumble. "We'll be able to see the Irish coast soon enough," Jonathan told the young girl. "That should be exciting."

"I think I'm going to go have a quick bite to eat," Carrie announced. "Would either of you care to join me?"

"Not yet," Hannah protested. "I want to see Ireland."

"All right. Well, I'll catch up with you later." She placed a hand on Jonathan's arm, and he turned and looked at her, flashing an expression that said she should be careful. She nodded in understanding and headed off, her stomach still rumbling. She'd eaten most of her break-fast once she and Robert had settled the situation, but she still felt hungry for some reason.

In the dining salon, many of the other passengers chattered about how they'd be disembarking soon. A few mentioned the coast coming into view, and others seemed worried about the rumors they'd heard regarding German U-boats. One particularly boisterous gentleman said it was absurd to think the Germans would do something so bold, so crass. They hadn't torpedoed any other ships—why would they start with *Lusitania*? Carrie thought it was a good point until someone else mentioned that they may have torpedoed other ships in the past few days since they'd set sail and they just hadn't heard about it. The gentleman argued that the ship captain would know then and take good care of them.

Carrie hurried through her supper, not wanting to listen anymore. Once she was finished eating, she headed back out to the deck, absently wondering where Robert might be. She hoped his discussion with Constable Pierce had gone well and that Victor Anderson would finally get what he had coming.

21

Robert might've been pacing if there'd been any place to walk in Constable Pierce's small office. Though the man had been there when Robert had first arrived, over an hour ago, he'd rushed off to go help some of the other security staff manage an urgent problem. He'd promised he'd be right back, but then, there really was no way of knowing how long these situations may take.

Instead of pacing, Robert sat in a chair across from the constable's desk, tapping his fingers and trying not to fidget too much. He had to have checked the time on the clock above his head and his pocket watch a thousand times.

Finally, the door opened, and Constable Pierce bustled inside, muttering under his breath about, "damn Germans," and taking his seat. "Now, Mr. Crawford. I do apologize for taking so long, but can you tell me precisely what happened with Mr. Anderson this time? From your perspective? I managed to speak to the young lady as well."

Robert took a deep breath, trying to compose himself

The constable continued. "The young lady, Martha Hildegard, came by quite early this morning to tell me what happened. I'm already considering bringing Mr. Anderson up on formal charges. He could potentially end up locked up over this if the Hildegards intend to take it seriously, and I believe they will."

Robert let that settle for a moment before he dared to open his mouth. So… when someone like Carrie was attacked by a man, it was simply a matter of telling him to knock it off, but when someone with money like Martha Hildegard spoke up, well, suddenly it was worth listening to.

"Jonathan Lane and I were out for a walk. We came across Victor Anderson pushing a young woman up against a wall, manhandling her. She told him to stop several times, but he wouldn't take no for an answer, so I punched him in the face, simple as that."

That summed it up well enough, in Robert's opinion, so he sat there for a few moments staring at the constable, waiting for him to say something. Either he'd think he was being petty and ridiculous or get angry that Robert had been so direct.

Eventually, the constable's face cracked, and he began to laugh hysterically, banging his open palm on the desk hard enough to make it shake. Robert stared at him in wild confusion.

"Well, I guess that basically sums it up, doesn't it?" Pierce said. "Right to the point, isn't it?"

Nodding, Robert said, "Yes, I guess so."

"All right then." He picked up a pad of paper and scribbled a few notes down, muttering to himself the whole time. It didn't take long, and then, he stood, offering his hand. "Thank you for coming back down, Crawford. I hope that we can make it the rest of the way to Liverpool without any more incidents."

"And what of Anderson?" Robert set his hands on his hips, studying the man across from him.

"I'll file a report with the authorities as soon as we reach the coast. I have another matter I have to speak to them about." He dropped his eyes and shook his head, giving Robert the idea that whatever this is, it was far worse than the situation with Victor Anderson. "Damn Germans," he muttered again.

"Well," Robert began, clearing his throat. "I'll let you get back to other matters. Thank you again."

"Yes, thank you, Mr. Crawford." He patted Robert on the shoulder, but just as his hand almost reached the doorknob to open it for him, Pierce stopped. "Oh, and Crawford... be careful."

His eyebrows furrowed, Robert stared at him for a moment, a question forming on the tip of his tongue, but he didn't ask it.

Studying the older man's face, Robert got the idea that he wasn't talking about the situation with Victor. No, he was implying something more sinister for certain.

Wondering what he knew, Robert nodded and headed down the hallway, thinking he should try to find Carrie. He knew from the last time he'd checked the clock that it was well past lunchtime. She was probably back in her room reading or sitting on the deck looking at the Irish coast.

The thought had him increasing his speed a bit. They were getting awfully close to Ireland, which not only meant they'd have some beautiful views of the coast but that they needed to be more diligent. It wouldn't make much sense for an enemy U-boat to go chase a speedy passenger liner down in the middle of the open ocean, but here, where they'd have to slow down a bit because of the proximity to land, there was a better chance of something nefarious happening.

He took the steps two at a time when he could, until he got caught behind a family going far too slowly for his liking, chatting along the way. A little boy kept asking questions about when they get back to England, and every time his mother turned to answer, she'd stop moving, and the whole family would simply stand there, blocking the way.

By the time Robert was within one flight of stairs of the hallway that led to Carrie's room, he saw an older woman standing in the hallway with her hands under her chin, tears streaming down her cheeks.

Sighing, he turned and looked up those stairs, thinking this really wasn't his concern, and he should go stand near a lifeboat with his arms wrapped around Carrie just in case the unthinkable happens.

Or he could help this poor elderly woman who was clearly lost.

Knowing what he had to do, he placed a smile on his face and carefully approached her. "Excuse me, madam?" She was dressed in a nice outfit, though nothing fancy, so he thought she might be a Second Class passenger. "Can I help you?"

With wide brown, tear-filled eyes, the woman looked up at him. "I can't find my room," she whimpered. "My daughter... she'll be wondering where I am."

"It's no problem," Robert assured her. "I'm happy to help you. Do you remember what room you were staying in?"

She rattled off a room number he thought might not actually exist, but taking his best guess, he began walking down the hallway, hoping she'd see something familiar.

They changed directions several times, going up and down flights of stairs, turning corners, and not seeming to ever get any closer to the room she insisted was the correct number. Robert tried not to get too impatient with the tiny, frail woman, but the idea that he needed to get to Carrie continued to niggle in the back of his mind.

At one point, they turned a corner to see a couple of boys coming down the stairs from one of the decks above. "I swear, I did see something in the water," a young man was saying. "It was moving so fast, I couldn't tell if it was a machine or a fish, but it was huge."

"Nonsense, you didn't see anything," a young man with a British accent said, grabbing his mate by the collar and giving him a tug. The first fellow threw his elbow, and then they nearly collided with Robert, who was doing his best to shield the older woman from the mischievous boys.

"Beg your pardon, sir," the taller of the two said.

Robert shook his head and motioned for the boys to go on, and they hurried on down the hallway. In the meantime, Robert spotted a couple at the other end of the hallway who seemed to be looking for something–or someone. Their heads darted around every corner as they rushed along.

When the woman's eyes lifted and landed on the woman at his side, her expression shifted. Tugging her husband's arm, she said, "There she is! Mother!"

"Louise!" The little old woman picked up her pace as she rushed to her daughter. Robert still wasn't walking at his normal pace despite her rush.

When the two women finally met, they wrapped their arms around one another. "Where have you been, Mama?" Louise asked.

"I couldn't find you," the mother sobbed.

"Thank you, sir," Louise's husband said, extending his hand. "We've been looking all over the ship for her."

"It's no problem. She wasn't quite sure of her room number, but I wanted to make sure she wasn't alone."

The man started to say something, but Robert was in too big of a hurry to stand there and listen to the man tell him how grateful he was for returning his mother-in-law. Robert didn't need that many accolades in his life.

What he did need to do was to find Carrie.

Turning around, Robert hastily waved over his shoulder and then headed back toward the stairwell the two boys had been rough-housing on a bit ago. He thought he knew where he was at this point well enough to know where to go, once he was above deck and could look around the outside of the boat. While the outside of the *Lusitania* was large, inside, she was full of mazes with hallways and corridors that twisted and turned and what seemed like thousands of flights of stairs. He could see someone easily getting turned around if they weren't good with directions or hadn't spent much time on a boat. He'd been on more voyages than he could count while working for Mr. Anderson and he still managed to get turned around. Even the sister ships weren't built exactly the same on the interior, after all.

Thinking of all the ships he'd been on had him thinking about one he'd been lucky enough to avoid–*Titanic*. Some of the men who'd died on that ship were friends–or business acquaintances anyway–of Victor's. He'd heard stories from survivors about how they'd resigned themselves to going down with the ship. Looking around him at the dark hallways and stairwells, Robert couldn't imagine what it would be like to be on a ship that was going under and trapped down here. At the moment, he was moving slowly, stuck behind another family again, but he couldn't imagine the sheer panic of people running around trying to get out and then making it on the deck only to find out there was nowhere to go.

Robert saw the light of day shining down the stairwell and let out a deep breath. They had to be fairly close to a deck if he could see the sun's rays. He was just about to follow the slow family out when he felt a tug on the back of his jacket. Turning around, Robert looked right into the eyes of a boy who couldn't have been more than ten years old.

"Excuse me, sir. Can you help me find my mother?" Tears welled in the young man's eyes as he begged for help.

Cursing himself for being so tenderhearted, Robert managed another fake smile. "Yes, of course I can. Now, don't you worry. She must be close by. When did you last see her?"

"I don't remember," he sobbed.

Inhaling deeply, Robert took him by the arm and led him down the first hallway they came to. "Look at all of these women," he nudged. "Do any of them look like your mother?"

"No." The boy shook his head and wiped his nose on his sleeve.

Impatience welled up inside of Robert as he wondered how he became the self-appointed relocator of the entire passenger liner. But then, he heard a woman shout, "Billy!" behind him, and they both turned to see a woman rushing toward them.

For the second time in only a few moments, Robert bore witness to a happy family reunion and then rushed off praying he could finally find Carrie.

22

It seemed to be taking forever for Robert to finish with the constable. After finishing her midday meal, Carrie went back out to the deck to stroll around and wait for him, but when he never showed up, she went back to their rooms to see if maybe he'd expected her to meet him there. She found them perfectly empty. With a sigh, she'd gone back up on the deck.

Judging by the position of the sun in the sky, she thought it had to be close to 2:00. A lot of people had gathered on the deck earlier to catch a glimpse of the coast of Ireland, but now, a lot of those people had meandered away. It seemed nothing exciting was going to happen that day after all. Soon enough, they'd all be in Liverpool. Then what? She'd spoken to Robert about his plans. He was going to go right back to New York. Would she see him again soon?

Her mind was on that when she heard a bit of a shout from further down the ship, and then a spray of water whipped up from below and the entire boat shook. Letting out a yelp of shock, Carrie grabbed the railing next to her with both hands. Just as the ship began to resettle in the water, she heard another sound from deep in the ship and then the deck beneath her feet rattled again.

Eyes wide with fear, Carrie tried to decipher what had just

happened. It all seemed surreal. One moment, she was standing there thinking about her future. The next, the only thing keeping her from falling miles into the cold water of the sea was shaking underneath her like something awful had happened.

"Wh-what was that?" she asked aloud to no one. The other people on the deck all looked panicked and shocked as well. A few people who had been standing near the spray of water were wet.

Then, she heard a word she'd been praying no one would ever have to say while she was on the ship. "Torpedo!" one of the men who'd been standing just above where Carrie thought the ship had been struck shouted. "Those bloody Germans have torpedoed us! A passenger liner!"

"A torpedo?" Carrie couldn't believe what she was hearing. All of this time, she'd brushed off the comments of other passengers who were afraid something of this nature might happen. Now, here they were in the midst of a tragedy–and she had no idea what to do.

Carrie's feet stayed glued to the deck as the people around her began to panic. They screamed and ran in all different directions, many of them shouting the names of loved ones. Below her, Carrie could feel the promenade shaking and wondered if there was a fire somewhere deep in the ship, or if that was simply the collected fear of almost 2000 people reacting all at the same time to what would likely be the event that claimed many of their lives.

"Robert," Carrie whispered. "Where the hell are you?" She continued to stand there on the deck with her hands wrapped around the railing, watching people flood by. Fathers ushered their families hurriedly toward the lifeboats. Stewards handed life jackets to anyone who didn't have one. Since Carrie's was tucked away safely in her room, she accepted one a man offered her and put it on, still not moving.

Ruth's words tumbled through her mind. "Eighteen minutes," she whispered. How long had it been? Not more than three or four. Still, her time was nearly a quarter gone, and she'd done absolutely nothing.

What would Robert want her to do in this situation? She vaguely recalled the conversation with him where he'd told her not to wait for him, to get on a lifeboat. She also remembered what Mr. Ashton had told everyone when he was in the middle of the Titanic sinking. He wanted everyone else on the lifeboats so he could take care of himself.

Carrie had a choice to make. She could start running around in circles like most of these other people were doing, shouting Robert's name, looking for Jonathan, or she could get her butt on a lifeboat and get the hell out of there like both of them would want her to do.

"Damn it," Carrie mumbled, looking around. While it seemed like a simple decision to make, it would have been even easier if Robert would materialize in front of her, and she could talk him into getting onto a lifeboat with her if there was space.

But that wasn't happening, and since going down the stairs at this point was akin to running into a burning building, she decided to figure out how to get off the boat safely.

By now, the ship was listing badly. Carrie hadn't noticed it while she was standing still, but with the first couple of steps she took, it was apparent that the boat was going down quickly. Yet, steam still poured from three of the stacks, propelling the *Lusitania* quickly through the water. There was no way they were going to be able to launch lifeboats at this speed. It wouldn't be safe.

Needing to take action, Carrie ran down to where the lifeboats were being loaded. All of them were leaning out away from the ship, and she was sure the lifeboats on the other side would be swinging over the decks. How would they launch them that way?

Ruth's gesture came to mind—the lifeboat spilling the people out everywhere. She ran over to where the closest lifeboat was being loaded and looked down. "We're going too fast!" she muttered. Running over to the workers manning the lifeboat, she said, "It's going to spill!"

"Get out of the way, lady," one of the uniformed officers shouted at her. "We've gotta launch this boat. It's full."

"But it's going to dump everyone into the water!" Carrie looked up and locked eyes with a nervous looking woman with her arms around two small children. "Hold onto the seat!" she shouted. "The seat! Hold onto it!"

The woman's eyebrows furrowed just as the front of the lifeboat began to tip toward the water. Everyone inside screamed as the little boat quickly pitched forward. The men lowering her into the water shouted at one another, trying to lower both sides at the same time, but the speed of the passenger liner wouldn't allow their corrections to help the poor people in the boat who were quickly dumped right into the cold sea–all except for the woman and her two children whose hands were wrapped around the bottom of their seat. Carrie watched as the mother let go with one hand and tossed the children behind the boat. It hit the water, tossing her out of the ship, but then, when it fell back to bob on the surface of the Irish Sea, the two children were still inside.

"No!" Carrie shouted, watching the spot where the woman had gone under. She leaned over the railing, praying she'd pop out of the water as so many others who'd fallen had done, but she couldn't see her anywhere.

"Mama!" the two children shouted as other people who had tumbled out of the boat tried to crawl back inside. A few made it, but they were so cold from the freezing water, Carrie didn't know what their chances were of actually surviving.

"The lights are out!" People began to scream as they ran by. "It's pitch black down there!"

A lump formed in Carrie's throat as she turned toward the closest stairwell. No one was coming out of there now. Where the hell were Robert and Jonathan?

"Miss, they're loading more boats down there," one of the crew members told her. "But Captain Turner has given orders for us not to launch anymore until the ship slows down. You should go down there, claim your spot." He gave her a meek smile, one that told her he was trying to save her life even though he was fairly certain his was almost over.

With tears in her eyes, Carrie reached over and grabbed his arm. "Thank you. Best of luck to you."

He nodded solemnly, and she took off walking as quickly as she could toward where the next boats were being launched.

Walking uphill while leaning hard to her left side, it took her a few minutes to get there, but when she did, she'd arrived just in time to help an elderly woman into the boat. Her husband stood there, fretting over her. "What about you, Arthur?" she asked. "I don't want to go on without you."

"Someone has to tell the grandbabies Arthur Murphy died a brave soul," he said with a chuckle that was meant to make his wife smile but only made her cry.

"It's okay," Carrie assured Mrs. Murphy. "There are other boats. Please, get in."

"But I'm scared. The other boats fell," the older woman pointed out. Someone behind them ran by screaming, and Carrie turned her head to see a woman who was so panicked she'd run right past the lifeboat.

"They're going to wait until it's safer," Carrie assured her. Just behind them, she heard a crew member shouting to go ahead and lower the boat. She thought that went against the captain's orders and didn't appear to be too safe, but she was done trying to interject. "Come on."

With that, Mrs. Murphy kissed Arthur goodbye and got into the boat.

"You can get in, too, Miss," one of the workers told her.

Carrie looked behind her and saw that the lifeboat was almost to the water now with no incidents. It made her less afraid to get in. But then, the water wasn't nearly as far away now as it had been only a few moments ago. How long had it been? Ten minutes? Was their time halfway up?

A scream erupted behind them. Carrie turned to see another lifeboat lowering right on top of the one that had just made it down. "Oh, my God!" She covered her mouth with both hands as the second boat fell right on top of the first one, sending that lifeboat under the water and crushing anyone who was aboard.

She turned to lock eyes with the crew member who had just told her to get in.

"We'll... be more careful," he said, but Carrie knew he couldn't promise anything.

Taking a step back, Carrie looked around. They were beginning to load another boat not too far away, and most of the passengers on deck were still running around, screaming, looking for loved ones or just losing their minds such that they were not going to be able to navigate getting onto a lifeboat at all.

"I think I'll catch the next one," she told him. He shook his head but didn't argue with her.

As soon as they began to lower the boat, Carrie moved on to the next one. She used the railing to move herself along, afraid she'd tumble over and into the water if she didn't hold onto something. With every passing second, the ship was taking on more water. It wasn't going to be long now until the entire floating monstrosity was lying at the bottom of the ocean.

"Come on, children!" a woman was saying as she herded a group of youngsters along. "Let's get on this little boat where we'll all be safe."

"Mama! I'm slipping!" one of the little girls shouted.

Carrie let go of the railing and scooped her up. Her mother's eyes widened. "Let's go." Carrie grabbed the hand of another child and walked with the mother to the lifeboat, knowing she'd make sure this family got aboard–even if she didn't get on yet herself.

"Where are you Robert?" she muttered.

The mother climbed into the boat, and Carrie handed her the children. "Thank you so much."

Carrie nodded. "Good luck to you."

"Anyone else?" the officer in charge of the boat shouted.

Looking around, Carrie saw no one familiar to her. Was now her chance to keep her promise and get off the ship–or should she wait for Robert?

23

Robert had made it about halfway up the stairwell he'd vacated to help the little boy when a vibration rocked the entire ship. His hand happened to be on the railing at the time or else he might've lost his balance like a couple of other people around him. He caught a woman and helped her regain her footing as everyone in the crowded stairwell let out a gasp and then began to discuss what had just happened.

"Do you think we threw a propeller?" someone behind him asked.

"I don't know." The woman's voice that answered sounded bewildered. "What in the world?"

"Perhaps we've run aground," a man further up the row of stairs said. "We were awfully close to the Irish coast earlier."

"That's simply not possible." Another man, standing in front of him, turned to argue. "We are in the middle of the straight. The ocean is miles deep here."

"Actually, it's not all that deep." This voice came from behind him. An elderly woman, from the sounds of it, but Robert didn't turn to look. He didn't care.

What he did care about was getting the hell off that stairwell before the situation got worse, and everyone seemed to have stopped to discuss what might've just happened. "Pardon me," he shouted, already moving forward around the woman whom he'd righted a moment ago. "I need to get up to the deck."

"Yes, yes," the ocean depth expert replied. "We all do."

"Then turn around and walk, or I'll have to press past you." While he'd spent the last hour or so helping people, the tiny voice in the back of his head that said something awful had just happened was sounding an alarm, and the last thing he wanted to do was stay down below deck when there was a good chance the ship was going down.

For all the speculating about what that might've been, Robert already knew. He was no war expert, nor did he have a lot of experience with emergencies while out on the open ocean. Yet, with all of the discussion of what might be happening, he had no doubt what had actually occurred. The only thing he could think about at the moment was getting out of that dimly lit stairwell and up to the surface so he could have a look around at the situation and decide what to do next.

He'd almost made it past the group of people standing on the stairs and up to the next flight when the electricity flickered–and then went off completely, leaving them all standing in the dark.

"Oh, no!" One of the voices he'd heard before filled his ears. "This can't be good."

"No, it really isn't," he agreed, more to himself than to the panicked group behind him. While the survival instinct within him had kicked in already, and Robert's first thought was to push his way up the stairs faster to the daylight he knew had to be waiting beyond the barrier at the top of the stairs, he couldn't do that.

Turning to face the group behind him, where he could hear squeals and heavy breathing, he said, "Listen, we need to make our way out of here as quickly and orderly as possible. We only have one more flight of stairs, and then we'll be on the deck."

"But we don't even know what's happening!" an elderly woman shouted.

"Yes, we do," Robert said, matter-of-factly. "The ship has been hit by a German torpedo. It's the only explanation."

His response made several people begin to panic again, but

Robert didn't give them time to fall apart. "Everyone, grab the railing and swiftly make your way up and out to the deck. There will be a lot of people stumbling around behind us, and we must move or get run over. As soon as you get to the deck, make your way to the lifeboats."

"How do you know that's what's transpired?" one of the elderly men questioned, his tone accusatory.

"Because there's no other explanation. Now, let's go." Robert turned around in the pitch black and reached ahead of him until he felt a shoulder. He gave the person a little nudge, and they began to walk up the stairs, carefully at first, but once they saw daylight ahead of them, and the stairs were better illuminated, they picked up speed. A few moments after the electricity went out, Robert emerged from the stairwell. He blinked a few times against the sunlight and rushed over to the side of the boat to see if he could determine what the situation was exactly.

All around him, people screamed, running in all different directions. He saw families, lone children, elderly people, and panicked mothers with their children scurrying about. Even a few lone men were rushing around, pulling at their hair, straightening their ties, looking like they were doing their best to keep it together, even though it was obvious there wouldn't be a lot of room on the lifeboats for the men—not at first anyway.

By the slant of the boat, it seemed like there wouldn't be a lot of time to wander and wait. The last time Robert had looked over the railing of *Lusitania*, he'd been quite a bit higher up in the air than he was at the moment. Not to mention he was tilted completely to his right side as he tried to make his way closer to the spot on the deck that he could see was wet. Something told him that even if he bent over to look down at the ship at that spot, he wouldn't be able to see any evidence of the torpedo having hit the ship because of how deep in the water *Lusitania* was now sitting.

When Robert reached the portion of the deck that was wet, he peered over the side and saw the ocean not that far below him. "Oh, my," he murmured, not sure what else to say. It was quite clear that this boat, and everyone and everything on it, was about to end up at the bottom of the sea.

With that realization, Robert turned around and took in the scene around him. Despite the fact that he'd come to grips with what had to have transpired the moment he felt the ship shutter around him, it all became very surreal as he scanned the chaos around him. While he'd already taken note of plenty of desperate people running in all directions, shouting, looking for loved ones, he hadn't realized just how far gone most of these people were. The wild, panicked looks in their eyes showed the sheer terror each of them felt as they considered what was about to happen to them, particularly those with children.

Knowing he had to do something to help everyone he could, Robert scanned the deck for the closest lifeboat that hadn't been lowered into the ocean yet.

About twenty yards away from him, some crew members were loading a lifeboat. Even at this distance, he could see the desperation on the faces of the men who were helping women and children climb aboard. While they were calmly functioning, doing their jobs, he could imagine that, in the back of their minds, they were thinking about what was about to happen to them. He knew he was, and he had a chance to get into a boat as soon as the women and children congregating nearby had loaded.

But he wasn't about to do that, not when there were so many women with youngsters still crowding the deck. "Ma'am!" he shouted, hurrying over to a woman who looked completely lost. She had a baby in her arms, and a little boy clung to her leg. "This way!"

When he touched her arm, she seemed to snap out of a trance. "My husband! I can't find him."

"It will be all right," he assured her. "I'm sure he'll want you to get your children to safety."

She nodded, but as he tugged on her arm, she continued to look around, lost.

"I'll assist you," he told her, giving her another pull.

"Mama?" the little boy said. "What's happening?"

"Come along." Robert knew they were all running out of time. If he didn't get her on a lifeboat soon, he wouldn't have a chance to help anyone else–including himself.

"Yes, yes," she said, shaking her head, and the two of them began to move, along with the children, toward the lifeboat–just as they began to lower it into the water.

"Oh, no," the woman muttered.

"It's not a problem. There's another one." Robert pointed further down the boat. "Let's go to that one."

Here, the crowd was thicker. Robert didn't hesitate to lift the little boy up into his arms. "Pardon us! She has a baby!" he told everyone who was blocking their path. Even though they were all in a rush, hearing those words seemed to part the seas, and he was able to move the family forward.

As they approached the next lifeboat, a roar went up behind them. Robert turned his head to see the lifeboat they'd just missed tipping precariously into the water. The occupants, as well as the people who'd just loaded them into the boat, screamed, and as the front part of the boat tipped closer to the water, a few people were dumped into the icy water.

Robert gasped and made sure the little boy in his arms couldn't see what was happening. "Good God," he mumbled. The boat continued to spill out its contents as it got closer to the ocean.

It was then that he looked out across the water around the boat and realized only a couple of lifeboats were actually floating upright, and they were pulling away from the boat. Either that, or *Lusitania* continued to propel her way through the water away from the initial scene of the disaster.

Seeing the boats was one thing, but it was the bodies in the water that made a chill go down his spine. People in life vests waved their arms, begging for help. Other people bobbed on top of the water, many of them face down. He could see several women and children and wondered just how many lifeboats had been dumped. Several of them were floating upside down on the water.

Immediately, his mind went to Carrie. Of course, she was smart enough to get on a boat as quickly as possible. He knew she wouldn't wait for him because they'd talked about it. But then, what if she got on a boat–and it flipped?

"Women and children!" the crew member in charge of loading the boat shouted, snapping Robert out of his thoughts. Right now, he was helping this woman and her family. "Come on." He made his way through the group of people standing around the lifeboat, towing the woman with her baby behind him as he carried the small boy. "In you go."

Robert handed the little boy to a woman who was already in the boat and then helped the mother in, holding her baby for her, and promptly handing her back. He said a quick prayer over the family and then helped another woman with her children get into the boat. Once it was loaded, he stepped aside, hoping these people stayed in the boat.

By the time the lifeboat was lowering into the sea, the water was high enough it only had a few yards to go. Thankfully, it made it into the ocean and began to drift away.

Robert turned and looked around him, wondering if there was anyone else he could help. In the distance, he heard a voice he thought he recognized. Peering through the crowd, he caught sight of a frantic Victor rushing along the deck, mowing over everyone in his way.

"Well, shit," Robert mumbled.

24

"Anyone else then?"

The man loading the lifeboat was looking directly at Carrie as he asked the question. A few men scrambled inside to take up seats the women rushing by didn't take notice of. With a big gulp, Carrie looked over her shoulder one last time. Could she get on this boat if everyone she cared about stayed on the sinking ship?

A familiar face came into view through the crowd, and Carrie's heart leaped into her chest. "Wait!" she shouted as she realized he wasn't alone. "Two seconds! Here comes a young woman!"

He turned and looked over his shoulder with an expression Carrie couldn't quite read. Either he was annoyed or just so nervous about his own fate he didn't seem to want to pause for anything, but then Hannah was there, Jonathan right behind her, and Carrie was able to help the young woman into the boat.

"Can you believe this?" Hannah looked into Carrie's eyes, a tremor of excitement showing there, not the terror Carrie felt welling up inside of her. "We got hit by a torpedo!"

"I know," Carrie assured her. "Sit down, sweet girl. Where's Mrs. Smythe?"

"We went back to where she had been sitting, but she wasn't there," Jonathan explained. "I hope she got in a lifeboat."

There was no time for Carrie to mention that even if she'd gotten in, that didn't mean she was safe. After all the boats she'd seen dumped or dropped on top of other boats, she was still apprehensive about getting in herself.

"Come on, Miss Carrie," Hannah said as the crew in charge of lowering the boat began to send it down.

"Get in, Carrie," Jonathan insisted.

She locked gazes with him and saw a changed man. The cool, calm, collected Jonathan she'd always known and loved was gone. Behind his eyes, she saw the feral, wild animal she knew he'd turn into as soon as she got into that boat. Just like the others running around in a panicked state, he'd be left to fend for himself, trying to find a way to survive, and he'd already had to do that once.

It really wasn't fair at all.

Shaking her head, Carrie said, "I'll stay with you. I need to find Robert."

A chuckle escaped his lips, one that hinted at the madness that was to come. "No, it's okay. Robert wouldn't want you to stay behind and look for him. You know that. Get aboard. I'll be fine."

She imagined that was just what Mr. Ashton had told Mrs. Ashton before he plunked her into the lifeboat.

"Now or never," the crewman told her.

Jonathan began to help her into the little boat, even without her consent. "Really, it's better this way. Besides, you remember what Ruth said. Time is almost up, Carrie."

She understood what he was getting at. If he were to find a way to keep himself alive, he couldn't be worried about her. Still, with all of the pandemonium unfolding behind him, Carrie felt wrong leaving him behind.

"There's room!" she noted. "We can squeeze you in." The boat was fuller than most of the others as the crew had done a good job of grabbing people who were running by and letting them in on the secret of the lifeboat's existence, something many of them had failed to note as they frantically looked for loved ones or simply got swept up in the fury of thousands of people running wild.

Jonathan shook his head, and she knew what he was thinking. "I can't."

"You can," she argued as the crew began to lower the boat. They were over the water now, but it was so close to the deck, he could still get on. "You're not taking anyone else's seat when no one is trying to get in."

He continued to shake his head, but then one of the ropes lowering the boat caught, throwing it off balance. Images from earlier when people went tumbling into the ocean filled her mind. Carrie grabbed onto Hannah who was screaming now, all the ideas of adventure gone from her mind as fear filled her every thought, no doubt.

The lifeboat banged into the side of the ship, hard. Someone's hand was crushed. The woman screamed in pain, and the lady next to her tried to help as the lifeboat careened closer to the boat again.

"Cut the rope, damn it!" Jonathan shouted. "It's already low enough. You're going to dump it!"

The rope slipped again, pitching them forward. The same chaos aboard *Lusitania* they'd all been fleeing filled their little lifeboat as the crewmen continued about their tasks as if they didn't realize they were going to dump everyone.

A wave bounced the lifeboat against the hull again, with a loud clank. "We're at the water!" Carrie shouted. "Just release us!"

"For God's sake!" Jonathan pushed one of the crew members aside who didn't fight him as he pulled a knife from his pocket and began to saw through the rope that was preventing them from leveling out. It took him a few moments, but he managed to cut the lifeboat free just as the crew got the other side loose from the lowering mechanism. By now, the *Lusitania* had sunk so much, Jonathan was only a few feet above her head.

"Come on!" Carrie shouted to him as the rope began to slip from its pulley. "Ride the rope down!"

Other people in the boat also encouraged their savior to join them. "You saved us!" a little girl yelled. "Please—we need you!"

Jonathan didn't have much time to think with the rope slipping through the pulley, but when he locked eyes with Carrie and she gave him a pleading look, he cursed under his breath and rode the rope down until it slipped from his fingers, and he landed in the lifeboat on top of one of the crew members who was in the lifeboat to help them row.

The other man helped Jonathan right himself, and the woman next to Carrie said, "Here, sir. Sit next to your wife and little girl." She scooted over and made room for him.

Seeing no reason to argue, Carrie patted the spot. "Join us."

With a sigh, Jonathan sat down next to her and wrapped his arm around Carrie who still had her arms around Hannah. "You did save us," she reminded him in a whisper as the few men aboard with oars began to pull them away from the passenger liner.

Shaking his head, Jonathan swallowed a lump in his throat. "Just doesn't seem right, that's all."

"There's nothing right or wrong about any of it," Carrie replied. "Hundreds, maybe thousands, of people are going to die today. We don't get to decide who they are." Visions of Robert filled her mind again, and she tried her best to picture his smiling face in other circumstances. Jonathan had been right to tell her to get on the lifeboat because Robert would want her to do that. But her friend couldn't be hard on himself for taking a spot no one else was trying to fill.

"How long has it been?" Jonathan asked her. "Fifteen minutes?"

"Thereabouts," Carrie surmised. She thought about what Ruth had told her. Eighteen minutes was almost up.

Lusitania continued to take on water. It was difficult to keep an eye on the sinking vessel as the lifeboat pulled away. The crewmen were talking as they rowed. "We need to get away so she don't suck us under," one of them said.

Shaking his head, Jonathan said in a quiet tone that only Carrie and maybe the women around them could hear. "That's a myth. They aren't trying to get away from the sinking ship. It won't pull them under, and they know that."

"Then what are we rowing away from the ship for?" she whispered back.

He took a deep breath. "The moment *Lusitania's* deck goes under, there are going to be over a thousand people in the water, and they'll do anything to stay alive. Right now, it's unorganized chaos on that deck as people hunt for their loved ones, thinking they have more time. The lifeboats on one side are clanking against the side of the ship, and the ones on the other are practically useless because they're nearly floating on the water before they can get filled. We didn't have enough time."

She understood then. He was saying when those people found themselves floating in the frigid ocean water, they'd do whatever it took to save themselves, which included swamping the lifeboats and knocking the people sitting in them into the ocean to take their spots.

Carrie couldn't blame anyone if that happened. She would likely do the same. It was instinct to try to save oneself, after all.

As the lifeboat pulled further away, it turned slightly, and she was able to see the other side of the boat, the starboard side. There, the lifeboats were completely useless as they clanked against the hull. A few of the crew members were still trying to get them in a position where they could be loaded, but at this point, Carrie realized the best thing for them to do would be to release the lifeboats, drop them into the water empty, and pray that people were able to get into them once the ship went under—which wouldn't be long now.

"It's going down." Hannah's voice was weak now as the excitement she'd felt earlier was replaced with mortification. "There are still people on there. Lots of them. And kids."

"I know." Carrie tightened her grip on the young girl.

"Why didn't they get onto a lifeboat?" Hannah wanted to know.

"Some of them didn't have time. Others are still looking for loved ones." A tear began to trickle down Carrie's cheek. In front of her, a man jumped off the back of the ship and began trying to swim toward them. He was shouting for help as he swam, his life vest keeping his head above water.

He only made it a few strokes before the frigid temperatures had him sputtering.

"We should go back and help him," Carrie said loud enough for the crew members to hear.

No one acknowledged that she'd even spoken.

Jonathan squeezed her hand. "They won't," he told her. "Once the chaos dies down, they might go back and see if they can pull a few people out of the water, but probably not in time to save anyone."

"Where are the other ships?" Hannah asked. "Won't there be ships coming to save us?" A large wave rocked their boat, and a few women screamed, afraid they'd tumble out. They'd been lucky no one had fallen into the water when the boat was off kilter earlier. If it hadn't been for Jonathan, they probably would have lost many occupants.

"They're on their way, I'm sure," Jonathan told Hannah. "But it'll seem to take forever."

Hannah let out a little whimper, and Carrie pulled her tight as a little child behind her began to cry. Another was calling for his daddy. The sound of weeping filled her ears, but it wasn't nearly as loud as the other noises she heard–the rush of water and the screaming.

Lusitania was running out of time, and all Carrie could think about now that she was relatively safe herself was where in the world was Robert. She prayed that he was sitting in one of those few other lifeboats bobbing along on the water, but something told her he wasn't.

If she knew Robert, he wouldn't be in a rush to take "someone else's" seat in a lifeboat either. No, he was likely up there, amidst the chaos, helping others, as the ground beneath his feet was quickly swallowed up by the angry sea.

25

"What in the world are you doing, Robert old boy?" Victor asked, a maniacal gleam in his eyes. "We're running out of time. You can't just stand here! You've got to get into a boat."

Robert stared at his former employer for a few minutes, not sure what to say. Of course, he realized they were running out of time, but there were still plenty of women and children on the *Lusitania*, and he wasn't about to take one of their spots when he was a full-grown man.

Something told him Victor didn't much care about that. In fact, Robert was a little surprised Victor was still on the ship.

"Come along!" Victor grabbed him by the arm and started leading him toward another lifeboat that was being filled. "I'll pay our way in, and then, when we get back to dry land, you'll be my liegemen again. Just like old times, huh?" He patted Robert hard on the chest.

Pulling his arm free, Robert said, "No, thank you."

Victor stopped in his tracks and stared at him like Robert was the crazy one. "What do you mean?"

"I mean, I'd rather drown or freeze to death in the Atlantic than ever work for you again, Victor. I wish you good luck, but I will not be going with you." With that, Robert turned and took a few steps away.

"Ha ha!" Victor's laugh sounded deranged. Robert couldn't help but turn and look at him. "You're psychotic! You'd rather drown or freeze? Fine. Do it then. You were a lousy servant anyway. Good riddance to you."

Saying nothing, Robert simply stared at him, wondering if God might use this opportunity to show Victor Anderson the error of his ways.

But the millionaire didn't stand there long. Instead, he pivoted on his heel and headed over to the man in charge of lowering what would probably be the last lifeboat into the water. The promenade was so close to going under now, there wouldn't be much time.

Remembering what Carrie and he had discussed about there not being many minutes to spare, Robert knew he needed to come up with a plan to survive this once the boat beneath his shoes was no more, but curiosity got the better of him. Watching Victor Anderson approach a desperate man trying his damnedest to do his job even in the midst of utter chaos was almost as entertaining as watching a Vaudeville act. Victor pulled several large bills from his pocket and showed them to the man. He glanced at him once and shouted, "Lower away!" to his crew.

Victor threw a fit, stomping his foot, and holding the money up right to the poor man's nose. He only looked away, the calm serene expression on his face showing he'd already accepted his own fate and wasn't about to help a man for money he'd never be able to spend.

Shaking his head, Robert turned around and surveyed the situation. He was startled to see just how far down the ship had sunk. He only had to take a few steps back the direction he'd come to have the cold water of the Atlantic wetting his ankles.

"This isn't good," he murmured, looking out over the scene around him. Because he was on the side of the ship with the severe list, he felt like he was almost alone. A crowd had gathered on the back side of the ship, particularly on the starboard side where he believed the ship must be sticking out of the water. If he stayed here much longer, he'd be floating.

He didn't have a lifebelt, and going to find one at this point would be futile. He could swim well enough, but the Irish coast in the distance was way too far for anyone to swim in these conditions. The water was too cold. No, it wouldn't be drowning that would claim most of these people. They would freeze to death within a few moments of going into the water–much like the poor souls aboard *Titanic*.

The scene around him was confirmation. Even though the ship had only begun to go down about fifteen minutes ago, there were plenty of people floating in the water who were no longer alive. Most of them wore life vests, but it didn't matter. The frigid water temperature had been their undoing.

His eyes grazed over the boats bobbing on the water. More of them were upside down than right side up, it seemed. At least, that was the scene right in front of him. From this distance, he couldn't see any of the individuals sitting on the lifeboats that drifted along like corks bobbing up and down in what was a relatively peaceful body of water considering it was about to consume several hundred people. But he imagined Carrie was out there now, probably wringing her hands and praying that he was okay.

He had to find a way to be okay.

"Listen, I've got another plan!"

Victor's voice bit into his eardrums the same way the cold sank its teeth into his ankles. Robert didn't even want to turn around and look at him.

The millionaire ran right past him, holding up a wad of cash. "I'm going to swim to that lifeboat over there and get them to let me on." He pointed at the closest lifeboat that had people in it, but it was far too great of a distance for Victor to think he could swim in the freezing water.

"I don't think that's your best plan," he mumbled.

"Hush. You're just jealous that you don't have the money to do it yourself, and I'm no longer offering to save your sorry ass." Victor stopped to glare at him for a moment then shouted, "Hey! Hey! You in the lifeboat! I have money!" With that, he leaped off the sinking promenade into the water and began attempting to swim toward the boat with his cash held up in his hand.

"Crazy bastard." Robert watched for a moment as Victor attempted to make a swim, but the offered money wasn't enough to make the people in the boat come back his direction. A few strokes into his swim, Victor essentially stopped moving forward, his movement slowing with every passing second.

Robert shook his head, wishing him well, but he couldn't continue to watch Victor try to make his way to the boat. He had to save his own ass.

The water was up to his shins now. Very little of *Lusitania* was still above water. No more lifeboats were being lowered on this side, and he imagined that the ones on the other side were probably too high up in the air and hanging at the wrong angle to be lowered down.

Then, he realized that the trajectory of the ship had taken it close enough to one of the lifeboats turned upside down and floating in the water that there was a possibility he could get to it. Whether or not he'd have the strength to turn it over, he wasn't sure, but he had to try. If nothing else, he could possibly climb on top of it and maybe pull up a few other people. When this ship went down, it would essentially leave probably close to two thousand people just floating in the ocean until they froze to death. While he had to prioritize saving himself for Carrie's sake, he wanted to be able to help others as well if he could.

Taking a few steps through the frigid water, Robert approached the railing and then swung his legs over, which wasn't hard since they were nearly submerged now. The moment the icy water made contact with his torso, all the breath left his body. A thousand pin pricks of pain stabbed him from his ankles to his shoulders. Gasping, he did his best to propel his body toward the lifeboat, but he wasn't moving quickly at all. He understood why Victor had only taken a couple of strokes before he seemed to practically freeze in place. Robert couldn't let the same thing happen to him.

A pair of stunning green eyes appeared in his mind's eye. The sound of her laughter echoed in his ears. The feel of her soft mouth pressed against his lips kept him moving even though every stroke seemed to take more energy than climbing an entire flight of stairs. Telling himself just to keep moving, he sliced his way through the water, telling himself it wasn't as cold as he thought it was, that he'd been in colder water, that he'd be fine. For all of his efforts, the pep talk wasn't doing him much good. The lifeboat seemed further away from his reach with every passing second.

But he was getting closer to it. Behind him, the screaming intensified, and he imagined more people were finding themselves with water lapping at their ankles. The reality of what was happening, of what was about to transpire, had to be sinking in now.

That wasn't the only thing that was sinking. Robert was so close to the disappearing ship, the fear that he might actually be sucked down with it made him try even harder to move through the unyielding water. While he was fairly sure that the idea of the ship creating suction wasn't true, at least not the kind strong enough to pull him under from where he was currently located, he didn't want to take any chances.

Robert took a deep breath and kicked as hard as he could, moving through the water in the same fashion a snail might cut a path through a river of maple syrup.

But he was making ground. He could see that now. Either that or the ocean was displaying a rare moment of kindness and was bringing the overturned lifeboat closer to him. In his estimate, he was about five strokes away from being able to reach it. But then, he'd have to find the strength to swim those few more strokes.

The noises behind him continued to intensify as screams, shouts, and splashing filled his ears. Robert had only one goal—get to the damn boat.

He could no longer feel his feet, and his legs were beginning to freeze up as well. His head slipped under the surface, and suddenly, he was more concerned with not drowning than reaching the overturned lifeboat. If he couldn't breathe, he couldn't swim.

"Come on, damnit!" he said aloud. "You can do this." Taking a deep breath, he spit out the water that filled his mouth and pressed forward, stretching his shaking arm as far ahead of him as he could. He knew that even when he was in or on the boat, he was still going to be soaking wet—and freezing cold. But he had to keep trying.

Finally, Robert's fingertips grazed the edge of the boat. It was the boost he needed to find the energy to pull himself over. Grabbing hold of the ledge, he tugged himself toward the lifeboat and did his best to tip it out of the water to flip it over. It was far too heavy, and he was in no shape to muscle it over. Instead, he used the little strength he had left to grab the top of the boat and haul himself as far out of the water as he could.

His first effort only managed to get him out up to his waist. HIs legs were still submerged in the frigid ocean. That wasn't going to cut it. With one more bout of concerted effort, Robert propelled himself up and out of the water. Panting and still freezing cold, he swung his legs up and over the top of the lifeboat.

It was then that he looked back at where he'd come from, expecting to see a sinking ship. Where the *Lusitania* stood only moments ago, there was nothing but a void.

She was gone.

And all that was left were hundreds of hundreds of people in the water—screaming, trying to swim—and freezing to death.

Robert wrapped his arms around his legs and did his best to warm up, but he knew that being out of the water didn't mean anything now. He was still too cold, and if another boat didn't come along and save him soon, he'd be just like them.

Freezing to death.

26

"We have to go back!" Carrie shouted only moments after *Lusitania* disappeared below the surface of the water. "Those people are going to freeze to death if we don't go help them—now!"

Her words seemed to fall on deaf ears as none of the men rowing the lifeboat even looked over their shoulders. They continued to row the little boat as far away from the site of the sinking as possible.

"We can't just leave them." Tears sprang to Carrie's eyes as she turned her head to watch the horrific sight unfolding behind her. Everywhere she looked, she saw people struggling in the water. Their white life vests glinted in the midday sun as they thrashed about, crying for help. Those who could attempted to swim to the closest lifeboat, while many couldn't make any traction in the frigid water and stayed where they'd first encountered the cold Atlantic of the otherwise tranquil sea.

"They won't go back," Jonathan said quietly. "Nothing any of us say will compel them to turn around and go back for people they think may swamp our little boat and have us trade them places."

"But there are children in the water." Carrie was thankful that she wasn't close enough to see the specifics of who it was calling for help, but it wouldn't be possible for every single child that had been aboard

159

the passenger liner to have made it into a life raft. No, some of those cries were coming from the littlest, weakest, and most fragile members of their cohort. They had all been a group of passengers united by the common goal of getting across the Atlantic together. Now, it was every man, woman, or child for him or herself, and it broke Carrie's heart to think that anyone could be so selfish as to continue to row away from children that were literally freezing to death.

Taking a deep breath, she attempted to pull herself together. A few of the other occupants of the lifeboat also agreed that they should return to help, but those with the oars continued to ignore them and sprinted ahead toward the Irish shore in the distance.

After a few moments, the man in charge gave an order, and the rowing abruptly stopped. For a few seconds, Carrie hoped that he had actually changed his mind and was about to tell the men to turn back and begin to assist those still struggling in the water. But that wasn't what happened. Instead, the little boat sat there bobbing on the waves, doing nothing at all.

"We'll wait here for rescue," the man in charge explained. "Boats will be coming from Queensland and other local towns."

"But what about them?" Carrie pointed back at the little specks of white in the water. Most of them had gone still by now, and only an occasional shout for help reached her ears.

"Nothing can be done for them now." His dismissive tone as he ran a hand through his black hair made Carrie want to pick her way through the crowd and push him into the water to see how he liked it, but that wasn't something she was capable of doing. Unlike some people, she couldn't sit idly by and watch someone freeze to death.

Or maybe she could. She was being forced to do just that.

"I hope Mrs. Smythe isn't out there." Hannah's voice was quiet and meek, unusual for the child. "Or your friend Robert."

At the mention of his name, Carrie felt her eyes prickle with tears once more. "I hope they are both safely on another lifeboat," she agreed. Jonathan's arm tightened around her shoulders.

Silence filled the lifeboat except for the occasional sob from one of the women, likely those who knew their husbands had gone down with the ship. Carrie sank her teeth into her bottom lip in an effort to keep her own emotions in check, but the tears escaped and slid down her cheeks. She didn't lift a hand to wipe them away.

"It shouldn't be too long," Jonathan whispered. He looked around and nodded. "Fishing boats in the distance."

Carrie turned her head and saw several boats making their way across the Atlantic. With the number of lifeboats that did happen to make it successfully into the water, she wondered how long it would take for it to be their turn. While she hoped some of those vessels would be able to help the people in the water, in the last few minutes, everything had gone eerily quiet from the area right around where the ocean liner had disappeared.

She had an idea there wouldn't be many bodies pulled from the sea—not living ones anyway.

Thoughts of Robert invaded her every thought as she watched the first rescue boats reach the survivors in a lifeboat not too far from their own. Could he be on that boat? Or maybe that one over there? She had no way of knowing. All she could do was pray.

Several hours went by in near silence. Only the sound of whimpering and the gentle lull of the water against the small boat kept Carrie tethered to reality as the horror of what had happened threatened to pull her under even further than a rogue tidal wave. She continued to remind herself that Hannah needed her, or else she might've let the dark thoughts tugging at the corners of her mind pull her under.

Finally, as darkness fell around them, the situation began to change. Slightly numb from the cold and horrible thoughts that plagued her mind, she blinked a few times when she heard Jonathan say her name. "It's our turn, love."

He nodded at an approaching fishing boat. Carrie took a deep breath for the first time in a while.

In an Irish brogue, a large man with a long red beard shouted, "We're comin' for you!"

Sighs of relief and cries of joy rang out around her. Hannah squeezed her hand, and Carrie kissed the top of her head. "We'll be safe and warm soon."

Unloading the lifeboat safely was a challenge in itself. Carrie waited patiently until it was their turn. Then, Jonathan lifted Hannah over to one of the fishermen. He asked, "Do you want me to pick you up, too?"

"No, it's okay," she assured him. With his help, she made the crossing onto the boat as the other women had done. By now, her legs were stiff, throwing her coordination off, but she managed to make her way onto the fishing vessel. The smell of a fresh catch filled her lungs with every inhale. Ordinarily, she'd think of this as an interesting adventure, but at the moment, every thought was filled with Robert's handsome face.

The fishing boat wasn't cut out to hold so many people comfortably, but then, everyone was already miserable, both physically and emotionally. Once everyone was loaded up, Carrie and her friends found a spot along the railing to hold on to as the boat turned and headed toward Queenstown.

Once again, tears threatened to spill from Carrie's eyes. It was all she could do to keep from crying her eyes out as she thought about everything they were leaving behind. It seemed surreal now to consider that just a few hours ago she'd been sitting in a nice dining room eating lunch, listening to dozens of other people chatter about what they planned to do once the ship reached Liverpool.

How many of those people were now floating in the water? Too many, that was for certain. But then, even one person would be too many.

She found herself sinking back into a bit of a stupor. While she was aware of what was transpiring all around her, it was as if she were watching life go by out a window. She saw the Irish coast growing larger, heard the fishermen and others around her talking about what they would do when they reached the harbor, even heard Jonathan make a few remarks in her general direction she assumed were for her, but none of it registered.

In her heart, all she could do was pray that Robert would be standing up there waiting for her, but the possibility seemed slim as they waited their turn to approach the dock and unload. Only one boat could approach at a time since the dock was so small. Some of the lifeboats had been towed in while others, like theirs, had had all of the passengers transferred to the fishing boat.

The citizens of Queenstown had come out in droves, it seemed, to help them all. A large number of women waited for them, some with food and blankets, others with water or just a hug and a few words of encouragement. Men helped them disembark. Carrie nodded a thank you to the older gentleman who helped her step onto the dock, but her throat was too dry for her to form any words.

"Let's get these survivors to the hotel," a middle-aged woman in a nice dress directed. Something about her gave Carrie the impression she was important. She was certainly taking charge. On numb legs, she followed along, accepting a piece of fruit and some water from another volunteer as she trudged onto dry land.

Amidst the shouts of their new hosts giving directions and calling for assistance, Carrie heard bits and scraps of conversation from her fellow passengers as well. The common refrain seemed to be, "Where is my husband?" or "Have you seen my father?" Those who didn't need medical attention fanned out in all directions looking for loved ones while the volunteers encouraged them to go to one of the shelters they'd put together first to see if perhaps a sweet reunion may happen there.

Without the strength to put up a fuss, Carrie continued to walk along, holding Hannah's hand, with Jonathan's arm around her. Even as they made their way to the hotel, she couldn't help but look around, searching the hollowed faces of the other people rescued from the disaster for the familiar brown eyes of the man she loved.

Robert was nowhere to be found.

"Let's get some rest, and then we'll be able to look for him properly tomorrow," Jonathan suggested. "It's dark and chaotic. Hannah is freezing."

Carrie nodded in agreement, but it was difficult to accept the fact that she'd probably lay her head down that night without knowing whether Robert was dead or alive.

"What's going on over there?" Hannah pointed off in the distance where a couple of men were transporting a figure wrapped in a sheet to one of the nearby buildings.

She opened her mouth to reply, but all that came out was a stuttered whimper.

"Some of the people in the lifeboats fell in the water first, remember?" Jonathan said calmly. "They must've been too cold."

"You mean they're dead?" Hannah asked him, looking up with tears in her eyes.

He nodded. "Yes, Hannah. They're dead."

She bit her bottom lip and nodded, tears escaping down her cheeks. "I will say a prayer for them."

"That's a good idea." Jonathan patted her gently on the shoulder. "Come along now. We're almost at the hotel. We'll get some rest, some food, and find the people we're missing in the morning."

Knowing there was nothing more they could do at the moment, Carrie followed along. Inside, the hotel was crowded with people from other lifeboats. Her eyes searched the crowd. She'd almost given up hope of seeing anyone she knew when her eyes fell on a familiar face. Letting out a deep breath, she thought, *Well, at least one of our prayers was answered.*

27

"Mrs. Smythe!" Hannah let go of Carrie's hand and ran across the hotel lobby to embrace the older woman who was sitting in a chair looking forlorn and half-frozen to death.

Hesitating for a moment, Carrie watched the scene unfold. Of course, she was overjoyed to see that Mrs. Smythe had made it off the ship alive, but if she was going to find a familiar face in the crowd, that was not the one she longed to see. Her eyes panned the crowd, but she didn't see anyone else she knew.

Jonathan approached them. "I'm so glad you were able to find a seat on a lifeboat," he told the older woman. "We were worried, but we couldn't find you."

"After the torpedo, I got up to look for Hannah, but I didn't see you anywhere, and a gentleman offered to help me into a boat, so I went. There was no way a woman of my age was going to survive in that water. I thought a responsible gentleman such as yourself would find a way to get Hannah on a boat. I see that you managed to get yourself on one, too."

The judgment in Mrs. Smythe's voice had Carrie swallowing hard. Why would someone say something so cruel? Jonathan blinked a few times, and Carrie recognized that guilty expression beginning to creep onto his face.

Hannah explained the situation in a proper tone. "Mr. Lane had to get on the boat. The front was lowering far too quickly. He leaped down and cut us free, and everyone insisted he get in with us." Her explanation left no room for arguments.

Before Mrs. Smythe could reply, a woman dressed in a uniform came over. "We've got a room for you now, Mrs. Smythe," she said. "Oh, and I see you've found your charge. Wonderful." She turned and looked at Carrie and Jonathan. "Hello there. I believe we have a room we can put the two of you in as well. Would you and your wife like to follow me, sir?"

Carrie's mouth dropped open. It wasn't the first time someone had mistaken them for a couple. "We're not–"

"Yes, thank you," Jonathan said quickly. "That would be wonderful."

The woman smiled as Carrie raised her eyebrows at her friend. He shook his head dismissively, and the four of them followed the woman to a set of stairs that seemed to lead to the heavens. Her legs still a bit numb, Carrie didn't know if she'd make the climb, and Mrs. Smythe had even more trouble. They took their time, and Jonathan helped the woman who'd been so unkind to him.

Finally, they managed to reach the small room at the end of the hallway. Hannah and Mrs. Smythe were in the room across from them. The girl hugged Carrie and Jonathan and went inside with her governess, and Carrie wondered if she'd ever see her again. She hoped so.

"We've had some soup and sandwiches delivered. I'll see if I can find a change of clothing for you both and bring them over," the kind maid said.

Jonathan thanked her and she left, closing the door behind her.

"We're sharing a bed?" Carrie asked, looking at a mattress that barely seemed big enough for one.

"I'll sleep on the floor. I knew we needed to take whatever accommodations we could, Carrie. There are a lot of people still looking for rooms down there."

He wasn't wrong. The two of them sat down to eat, and Carrie realized just how cold, hungry, and tired she truly was. They devoured the food with little conversation. All she could think about was the others. Not just those waiting for a room, those who were injured, but also those who would never sit down for a meal again.

Mostly, though, she thought about Robert.

By the time they'd finished, the woman was back with some night-clothes and a change of clothing for the next day. She explained she'd done her best on the sizing. Carrie thanked her, and she left. For a moment, she lamented all the new clothing she'd lost, but that was nothing compared to what so many others had parted with.

There was no privacy in the small room, so the pair of them took turns stepping out into the hallway while the other changed. When Carrie let Jonathan back into the room, she said, "I think the floor will be quite uncomfortable. Do you think Edward will mind if we share the bed?"

He chuckled. "I think it will be the only amusing situation to come of any of this."

She laughed, too, and for a moment she let herself forget the horror of that day.

Back to back, the two of them lay down, sharing a blanket and what promised to be a night full of horrible dreams.

The next morning, Carrie awoke thinking it was odd the boat had stopped moving. Before she even opened her eyes, a flood of memories hit her, and she remembered she was no longer on a boat. The rocking sensation she'd grown accustomed to was faint now, a residual effect from being at sea. But she was on dry land now.

Sitting up, she couldn't help but say his name. "Robert!"

The room was empty. Where was Jonathan? She glanced around and saw the change of clothing he'd been given was gone. Knowing her friend, she imagined he was already out looking for Robert. That was just how Jonathan was.

Carrie got dressed and went downstairs, hoping to find a more peaceful situation than the one she'd witnessed the night before for everyone else's sake, but if anything, it was more chaotic. People wandered around the hotel lobby, most of them women, and many of them crying or asking anyone who walked by if they'd seen a loved one. One woman had a locket open and was asking about a little boy. Carrie's eyes filled with tears. How had the lady gotten separated from her son?

Out of nowhere, Jonathan appeared in front of her and handed her a small apple. "Good morning."

"Is it?" she asked dryly.

"Not in the least," he admitted. "Eat that, and then come with me."

"Can't I eat it and come with you?" she asked before taking a bite.

He shook his head. "No. Where we're going, you won't have any appetite."

She took a deep breath. "You didn't find him, did you?"

"No, but I haven't done much looking. I've been out asking questions, trying to figure out where he might be."

"And?" She swallowed and bit off another chunk, knowing she needed to eat, even if her mouth felt dry, and it was difficult to swallow.

"And what I've discovered is that we may not find him no matter what the circumstances are, not easily anyway. Some of the survivors were taken to other towns. And many of the… others… have not been located yet."

Bodies. He meant many of the bodies. She could only nod, not able to think about her sweet Robert as just that–an empty body. No soul, no life. No smile.

"They are laying out the less fortunate passengers and trying to identify them," he explained as Carrie finished her apple and looked around for a place to discard the core. She tossed it into a wastebasket and followed him out into the street.

The scene out here was much like the one in the hotel. Every-where she looked, Carrie saw weeping women and other lost souls wandering around looking for their loved ones. The closer they got to the area where the bodies were being laid out, the more bereaved the crowd became.

Despite the possibility of further confusing everyone they encountered, Carrie reached over and took Jonathan's hand. He gave hers a squeeze and pulled it up so that her arm was through his. The pair of them joined the queue of survivors looking over the faces of the lost.

The first body Carrie saw was a small child, and she nearly broke down in tears. His pale face, blue lips, and utter stillness seemed so hard to grasp. No one should have to die so young and innocent.

Jonathan moved her along quickly, their eyes rapidly moving from one departed soul to the next. With each new focus on facial features, Carrie tried to brace herself. What was she going to do if her gaze landed on a familiar face? What if she found Robert among the crowd?

She heard Jonathan's gasp before her eyes had caught up to his, and for a moment, she assumed the worst. But when her gaze finally shifted to the face of the man lying there, cold and stiff, it wasn't Robert.

It was Victor.

Despite despising the man, Carrie still gave a startled cry and covered her mouth with both hands. "Oh, God," she muttered, shaking her head. Even though he had treated her, and others, terribly, no one deserved to die like that.

"Do you know this man?" one of the volunteers from Queenstown asked.

Jonathan answered since Carrie couldn't form words. "Yes. That's Victor Anderson."

"*The* Victor Anderson?" someone else asked.

"That's right. The New York City millionaire from the affluent family," Jonathan continued. "We spoke to him many times aboard the ship."

"Oh, dear." The workers exchanged a look. "We'll need to notify someone."

Carrie didn't want to listen to the rest of their conversation. She hoped the notification had to do with identifying the body and not the fact that someone so rich had gone down with the ship, but she couldn't let thoughts of inequality fill her mind at a time like this. It seemed quite clear the Atlantic had no opinions when it came to station or how much money one was worth.

Still clutching Jonathan's arm, Carrie made her way through the collection of macabre forms, some of them in a ghastly state while others looked as if they'd just drifted off to sleep. When they were done checking that location, they went to another and then down to the docks where more bodies were being brought ashore.

When she couldn't find Robert anywhere, Carrie was grateful, but that didn't stop the longing in her heart. If he wasn't here, where was he? And could she continue to hope that he was alive?

A list had been compiled of all the people who'd been identified, and his name was not on it. Nor was he among the list of the living she'd put her own name on the day before. It seemed that Robert had just vanished from the face of the earth.

Later that evening, when they returned to the hotel, a fellow stopped them to let them know that transportation would be provided the next day. They'd take a train and then a ferryboat. Jonathan pulled her aside. "Do you want to go or continue to look?"

Tears welled up in Carrie's eyes. She'd come here to do a job, and she needed to finish it, but what if Robert was here somewhere and she'd just missed him? "I don't know."

"There's a chance Robert will be headed there as well," Jonathan reminded her. "After all, he knows that's where you were going."

He made a good point. Carrie nodded. "I think we should go then."

With a deep breath, Jonathan said, "We'll find him, Carrie."

"I know we will," she replied, but inside, she wasn't so sure.

With every passing moment, she was beginning to lose hope, and that was a dangerous thing.

28

Stepping off the ferryboat onto dry land was one of the most wonderful feelings Carrie had ever experienced. Even though she'd spent the last couple of days in Queenstown, getting back on the water had been terrifying. She'd spent much of the time clinging to Jonathan's hand wondering how he had ever managed to convince himself to get on a ship again after the first time this had happened to him.

At Liverpool, they made their way to the train station. Carrie spent much of the time looking out the window, dreading the long passage back to New York and thinking about Robert. Was he there, lying on the dock somewhere in Queenstown, and she'd just missed him? Or was he still floating in the water?

"Carrie? Did you hear me?" Jonathan's voice was rich with sympathy. "We'll be arriving in Southampton soon."

She jerked her head around to meet his gaze. "Sorry. No, I don't suppose I've heard much of what anyone has said to me these past few days."

"I understand." He inhaled, and she assumed he was going to say more, but then he didn't, and she had to assume that was because there was nothing more to say. They'd each been through their own personal hell the last few days. Of course, this wasn't the first time he'd gone through this. Carrie prayed it would be the last time for both of them. For all of her lofty ideas about exploring the world, once she found herself safely back in New York, she didn't think she'd ever leave town again except for possibly by motor coach or train. Even then, it would take some convincing.

For a moment, the plans she'd allowed herself to dream about when she was with Robert came back to her. She'd seen herself stepping away from taking care of Mrs. Ashton and the little ones to become a bride, maybe someday even a mother. Now, with Robert missing, she had to let go of those dreams. Tears threatened to spill down her cheeks, but she resolved herself not to let them. It seemed wrong to mourn for him when there was still a chance he was alive.

"Once we've collected Mrs. Ashton's things from her mother, I'll stop by and see if we have any telegrams," Jonathan said as the other passengers prepared to disembark. He'd had a sum of money in his pocket that allowed them both to buy traveling clothes, but the other people from their shared disaster were sitting near them in a mishmash of borrowed clothing from the kind people of Queenstown. Carrie felt thankful that she wouldn't have to face Mrs. Westmoreland dressed in something that wasn't her own.

"Have you heard from Mr. Ashton since you sent the original message?" Carrie remembered that Jonathan had sent word home the day before that they had survived, but she couldn't remember if he'd told her anything more.

He shook his head. "No, but I told them we would be in Southampton later today, so I'm hoping to receive word from them while we are there."

She nodded but couldn't think of anything else to say. As they prepared to disembark, Carrie had to wonder how in the world she was going to hold a conversation with Mrs. Westmoreland. Despite knowing what a terrible mother the woman had been to Mrs. Ashton, Carrie needed to act professionally, and she wouldn't be able to do that if she couldn't articulate a sentence.

The train pulled into the station, and the two of them waited their turn to disembark. Thankfully, Jonathan still seemed to have all of his wits about him. Perhaps he was used to this feeling–the sense of floating around in one's body that may or may not deserve to be alive. At any rate, she took his arm, and he led her about as if she were an invalid or a small child. He hired a car, and what only seemed like a few moments later, they arrived at the convalescent home where Mrs. Westmoreland resided.

"Carrie, are you well?" Jonathan asked before they stepped out of the vehicle. "I know Mrs. Westmoreland can be intimidating. While I intend to let you handle the situation since Mrs. Ashton appointed you to do so, I will be right there with you the entire time."

"I'm fine." She managed a smile, though she imagined it didn't look natural. He tipped his head slightly to the side in disbelief but still nodded before paying the driver, and the two of them got out of the motorcoach.

The smell of antiseptic hit her lungs the moment they walked inside. Nurses wearing white with large hats made their way down the corridor, carrying charts or pushing patients in wheelchairs. Carrie tried not to stare at the residents, all of them elderly, many of them looking out of sorts. She imagined one day she'd be in a place like this if she were lucky enough to live that long.

"May I help you?" The woman behind the counter off to the side had a sharp tone about her and a thick British accent, but her eyes were kind, giving her the sense of being someone who was caring but didn't have much time to spare.

Clearing her throat, Carrie called upon her memory to get her through. How many times had she rehearsed this conversation, and the next, on her way across the Atlantic? Too many to count. "Good day. We're here to see Mrs. Mildred Westmoreland."

"Are you family members?" she asked shrewdly.

"No, we are employees of her daughter, Mrs. Mary Margaret Westmoreland Ashton," Carrie explained. "Mrs. Ashton is with child and was unable to make the trip to meet with her mother."

"I see." The woman took a moment to flip through a binder on her desk before she nodded and said, "This way."

Relieved that she wasn't given any additional run-around, Carrie followed the nurse down several hallways, Jonathan behind her, until they reached what had to be Mrs. Westmoreland's room.

"Here we are." Pushing the door open for them, the receptionist nodded and stepped away, leaving Carrie staring into a dark room where she could only see the outline of a small form sitting in a bed amidst the shadows.

An overwhelming scent of lilacs rolled out of the room causing Carrie's eyes to water. She forced herself to ignore the smell, though, and stepped inside. Not sure whether or not Mrs. Westmoreland was even awake, she approached the bed.

"Who are you?" a gravelly voice demanded.

"Good day, Mrs. Westmoreland. I'm Carrie Boxhall, and this is Jonathan Lane. I believe the two of you have met. We are here on behalf of Mrs. Ashton."

"Who?" she demanded. "Mrs.--" She stopped abruptly and nodded. "Oh, yes. Meg." Mrs. Westmoreland was a tiny woman, frail, thin, with skin so white it nearly glowed in the darkness of the room. When she spoke her daughter's name, her mouth drew into such a thin line, it nearly disappeared.

"That's correct. She apologizes that she couldn't make it herself. She's about to give birth to your second grandchild."

Mrs. Westmoreland snorted dismissively. "I'm not entirely surprised my daughter did not come to see her mother on her deathbed. All these years, and she still has absolutely no respect for me. Well, it's no matter now." She turned her head toward the wall as if the conversation were over.

Carrie turned to look at Jonathan who shook his head slightly and bit down on his bottom lip.

Turning back to Mrs. Westmoreland, Carrie continued. "Ma'am, it's my understanding that you have a package for her?"

"For her." She didn't even turn her head. "I would give it to her, but she is not here."

"No, but we are here on her behalf and have traveled many miles over perilous seas to reach you." Irritation began to grow in Carrie's tone, no matter how badly she fought it.

Snickering, Mrs. Westmoreland asked, "Perilous?"

"Yes. Our ship was torpedoed by Germans, and many people did not survive." Her annoyance shifted into something else, overwhelming grief, and Carrie found herself becoming more demanding by the moment. "Now, if you will please give us whatever it is you intended to bestow upon your daughter, we'll make our leave and let you go on about your day."

"Does it appear as if I am far off from those you lost at sea?" Though her neck was unsteady as she turned, Mrs. Westmoreland managed to focus her eyes on Carrie's face. "If you have any messages for them, let me know, and I'll be by to tell them shortly."

Taking a deep breath in through her nose, Carrie prepared to tell the wretched old woman what she thought, but before she got the chance, Jonathan said, "Very well then. Thank you for your time, Mrs. Westmoreland."

Carrie turned to shout at him, but then she saw him tucking something into his jacket and decided he must've found the package for Mrs. Ashton. It wouldn't be like him to simply walk away. "Good day, ma'am," she said before spinning on her heel and walking away.

They'd almost reached the door when Carrie heard the slightest whisper. "Tell her I love her."

She stopped in her tracks, her back straight, and turning to look at the woman, who was now facing the wall again, she said, "I will."

Then, the pair of them left, and Carrie hoped no one from their family ever had to see Mildred Westmoreland again.

Outside, Jonathan pulled a thick envelope from his jacket. "It was sitting on the nightstand with her name on it, so I figured we should save ourselves the trouble of trying to reason with the unreasonable."

"That makes sense," Carrie admitted. "Now, let's check the telegram and get out of here. As much as I hate the thought of getting back on a ship, I don't think they've created trains that go across the ocean yet, have they?"

"Sadly, no. We'll have to book passage home." Jonathan took her arm, and they walked to an area with shops until he reached the telegram station. She stayed outside while he went in to check.

While she was standing there, a boy came by selling newspapers, shouting about the *Lusitania* disaster. Carrie wanted to cover her ears, but when he said, "Survivors can be found in Liverpool!" an idea hit her.

Jonathan came out. "Mr. Ashton sends his regrets for our troubles and says they are all thankful that we are well." His eyebrows furrowed. "What is it, Carrie?"

"That boy," she began, not sure how to arrange her thoughts into sentences. "He is announcing that survivors are being brought to Liverpool."

"Yes, and?" Jonathan waited for her to continue.

"Well, what if I… tell the newspapers that I'm staying in Liverpool?"

Cocking his head to the side, he studied her face for a moment before saying, "I'm afraid I don't follow."

"What if we return to Liverpool, and I give an interview to the papers? I'm sure they're clamoring for anyone from *Lusitania* who is willing to speak. I don't want to do it, mind you, but if it's possible Robert might see the article and track me down there, well, it will be worth it."

Jonathan listened to her carefully, scratching his chin for a moment. "We would have to stay in Liverpool for a couple of weeks in order to make it worth the while, and there is always the possibility Robert is already on his way home to New York."

"I don't think he would've given up looking for me so quickly. He knows I had to come here. I think he would continue to search for me." What it was in her gut telling her this, she wasn't sure, but she was confident.

"All right then," Jonathan agreed. "We shall give it a shot."

"Thank you." For the first time in days, Carrie felt she had something to be hopeful about. The two of them headed back to the railway station to catch a train back to Liverpool where Carrie would do what she could to try to reach Robert.

If this didn't work, she had no idea what she would try next. She just might have been out of options.

29

Two weeks had crawled by so slowly, Carrie could almost count them as months. Every day, she and Jonathan would go out and check a new area of Liverpool for Robert. Every day, they would come up empty handed.

Speaking to the newspaper reporter had been difficult. Jonathan had explained that the pair of them would be willing to grant an interview so long as the questions were not too terribly invasive, and the reporter from the local paper had agreed. But once he'd begun to ask questions, they'd become increasingly intrusive until he was asking her to relive the events of the sinking, and she'd had to step away. Jonathan, who was normally so put together, had also stepped aside, telling the man this wasn't what they'd agreed to. He'd apologized and asked to try again, but Carrie told him he had enough for his story now and to be sure to state in the article that anyone who might be looking for her should contact him. The article had run in the paper the next day, and checking in with him had become part of her daily routine, but after fourteen days of coming up empty handed, with only other reporters from other papers reaching out to him to see is she was available to share her story with them as well, Carrie had to decide the gig was up.

"Just because we are going back to New York, that doesn't mean we have to stop looking," Jonathan reminded her as she stood near the window of her hotel room. They'd had very nice accommodations in Liverpool because of Mr. Ashton's bank account in England. He'd been able to authorize them to spend whatever they needed for the room, clothing, meals, and tickets home on any ship they chose. They could've secured transportation via Cunard, the owners of *Lusitania*, but the last thing Carrie wanted was to stand aboard a ship that looked like the very one she'd just seen slip beneath the surface of the sea forever.

"We should be leaving soon." He squeezed her arm gently. "The *St. Louis* leaves in less than two hours. As much as I don't want to climb aboard another passenger liner, I don't want to miss it either."

It took her a moment to respond as sadness welled up inside of her. She'd been so optimistic when she thought of putting the article in the paper, but her highest hopes had not come to fruition, and now, she was leaving with nothing.

The thought that it might be time to accept Robert had not survived crept into the corners of her mind, but Carrie wasn't ready to face it yet. Perhaps he'd hit his head and didn't remember who he was. Maybe he'd drifted to an island where there was no one to help him, but he'd be rescued soon. He could've been so severely injured he wasn't able to communicate his name to anyone. A thousand possibilities played over and over in her mind to try to explain away his absence without considering the most likely one of all—that Robert hadn't made it.

"Carrie?"

She realized she hadn't responded to Jonathan's statement. "Yes." She turned around. "Yes, of course. We should go."

He nodded and gathered the new bags they'd purchased. Neither of them had more than a few changes of clothing in them and a few necessities. Another memory of the fine clothes she'd bought for her trip flickered in her mind. They weren't important, but it was a reminder that nothing had turned out as she'd expected it to.

They took a hired motorcoach to the docks. The scent of fresh sea air which used to invigorate her made her stomach turn. A glance in Jonathan's direction told her he was struggling as well. How were they to endure a week's long voyage across the very sea that had tried to swallow them whole?

"Come along," Jonathan prompted once the car had stopped. "I know it's gut wrenching, but until aeroplanes are more reliable, and fit more people, this is the best we can do."

Despite her twisted stomach, Carrie let out a giggle. "Do you honestly think one day we'll all be flying around in the sky like a flock of birds?"

He shrugged. "It's already happening. Just wait and see."

Carrie laughed again, glad for the distraction. She had heard rumors of people using aeroplanes to get around, but the idea that one day just anyone would be able to climb into one of those large metal birds and take to the skies seemed like something out of a Jules Vern novel. It seemed just as frightening to be aboard a sinking aeroplane as it did to be on a ship going under, although she doubted there would be any chance of survival from falling from the sky.

With every step she took toward the *St. Louis*, her amusement faded. She gripped Jonathan's arm with her free hand and carried her bag with the other, wondering if he was as frightened as she was.

"Do you remember how Mr. Ashton didn't want to leave his room during our trips to and from Southampton together?" he asked in a somber tone.

"I do," she said, and before he could add more, she continued, "and now I think I understand why."

A chuckle rumbled in his throat. "Well, I managed to convince myself to spend time out in the open air on that voyage, but on this one, I may be locked in my room for the entirety of the journey. This might just be my last trip across the ocean."

Carrie hoped that wouldn't be because this ship also sank, but then, there were still German U-boats in the waters near Great Britain, weren't there? A shiver went down her spine. She never wanted to experience anything like that again.

Thankfully, Jonathan still had his wits about him enough to check them in and get them situated in their rooms. The accommodations were smaller, partially because they'd booked so late, but also because this ship wasn't nearly as luxurious as *Lusitania* had been. It would do, though, and Carrie decided to hang her spare outfits in the closet and try to pretend as if she were happy to be there. Was it really only a few weeks ago that she'd thought sailing across the ocean would be a grand adventure? Well, she'd had an adventure, all right, but not the kind she ever wished to have again.

A knock on her door startled her. She was used to Jonathan having an adjoining room, but this time, he was across the hall. She hoped it was him and not a steward or someone coming to check on her. She hated the idea of having to plaster a fake smile on her face and thank someone for providing such a nice room when all she really wanted to do was hide under the bed.

She opened the door to find her friend standing there with a nervous expression on his face. "I thought we should go out on the deck to wave goodbye to dry land."

"Why?" she asked, folding her arms. "In case we never see it again?"

He smirked. "It's considered bad luck to hide away in your room for the disembarkment, I believe. Besides, we should figure out where the closest lifeboats are and how they operate before we lock ourselves away."

That did seem like a good idea to her. There would likely be a muster drill later. Most ships had them now. But that wouldn't give them an opportunity to inspect the equipment. "That's a good idea," she admitted. With a sigh, she walked with him through the narrow hallways to the closest deck, memorizing the path in case she needed to know it in the dark at some point. Another chill went down her back. It was difficult not to put herself back in the position she'd been in on the *Lusitania* when she'd been so excited for their adventure.

Up on deck, a crowd had gathered along the railing. Lots of people were waving at loved ones standing along the dock. Even those who knew no one still had a fun time waving goodbye. Carrie twisted her hands together nervously, wanting nothing more than to go back to her room.

Jonathan led her over to the lifeboats, but she realized she had no idea what she was looking at anyway, so she let him do his inspection. A few times, he grunted, like he didn't approve of whatever mechanisms he had discovered.

Eventually, he stepped back to her. "I believe these are in even worse shape than the ones on *Lusitania*. Let's hope we don't need them."

All she could do was nod, biting back the first thought that popped into her head. Obviously, she hoped they did not need them.

While they were looking at the lifeboats, the ship had been pulling away. Carrie caught a glimpse of the port behind them, and an overwhelming feeling of sadness washed over her. She was leaving–without Robert. This wasn't what was supposed to happen.

Warm tears filled her eyes. She did her best to hide them, but Jonathan was the most perceptive person she'd ever met. "It'll be all right, Carrie. We'll find him."

"We won't if he's… gone." She couldn't bring herself to say that word. Dead. How could Robert be dead?

"I know you haven't given up on him." His tone was almost convincing.

Carrie managed a nod. She didn't want to believe she would never see the man she loved again, but it had been over two weeks. Maybe it was time to face the facts.

"Why don't we go…." Jonathan stopped talking, and his forehead crinkled. "Is that…?"

Carrie turned to look in the direction where Jonathan was staring. In the distance, she saw a tall man with dark hair wearing an ill-fitting suit, as if the clothes weren't his. Her heart skipped a beat. "Oh, my God!" Before Jonathan could even take hold of her arm, she rushed over, dodging people and weaving through the crowd toward the man who from behind looked just like Robert.

Eventually, she caught up to him. Grabbing him by the shoulder, she said, "Robert!"

The man turned around, and Carrie's heart sank. It wasn't him. The man's eyebrows raised in confusion. "Pardon?"

Gasping and trying not to cry–again–Carrie released the man's arm. "Oh, I'm sorry. I thought... I thought you might be–"

"Carrie?"

Her breath caught in her throat again. Was it possible? The voice from behind her sounded so familiar, and the way her name fell from his lips made her heart clench. Slowly, she turned around, afraid to even look at whomever had said her name. Getting her hopes up again only to have them dashed just might be her undoing.

With a deep breath, she lifted her gaze to meet a pair of warm brown eyes. "Robert?"

A smile broke across his handsome face. "It is you!"

Before he could say more, Carrie flung herself into his open arms. "Oh, Robert! I thought... I thought maybe you hadn't...." She still couldn't force herself to say the words.

He squeezed her so tightly, she thought she might break a rib, but she didn't even care as she locked her arms around his neck. "I've been searching for you. They took me to a small Irish island. I was in the hospital for a few days with frostbite, but then, I managed to get to Queenstown. It took a while to raise enough money from kind people in the town to catch a train and then the ferry to Liverpool." He released her enough so that she could look at his face. He looked tired and pale, but otherwise no worse for the wear. "I just got to Liverpool yesterday. I saw the newspaper, but by the time I got to the hotel this morning, they said you'd checked out. A kind man in the lobby overheard my conversation and offered to pay for my transportation back to New York. I was hoping we'd be on the same ship."

Tears slid down her cheeks. "I'm so glad you're all right. I've missed you so much."

"I've missed you, too." With that, Robert pressed his lips to hers, and all the fear and desperation she'd been feeling for the past two weeks faded away. Robert was alive, and she was never letting him out of her sight again.

30

The next few days passed by quickly despite the fact that no one in their party wanted to venture up to the deck for more than a few moments at a time and they took all of their meals in either Carrie or Jonathan's room. Robert was a steerage passenger, since he was there thanks to the kindness of a stranger. Carrie meant it when she said she never wanted to let him out of her sight again, so evenings were difficult.

One blessing for Carrie was that her stateroom did not have a balcony. While she constantly heard the sound of the water outside and felt the rocking of the ship, when she was in her room chatting with Robert, she could forget where she was for a time.

The further away from Europe they traveled, the safer she felt. War hadn't reached the United States yet, though she imagined the *Lusitania* disaster would probably have an impact on that, so when they were within one day of reaching New York harbor, she began to breathe a little easier.

The evening before they disembarked, she was sitting alone in her room with Robert, holding his hand and thanking God that he was all right. Despite his ordeal in the water, he didn't have any injuries that wouldn't heal with time. He'd gone over how he'd been about to slip back beneath the surface after hours of hanging onto an upturned lifeboat for dear life when a fishing vessel approached and pulled him and three other men from the water. After that, everything was a blur for several days until he awoke in a hospital and had to be reminded of what he'd endured.

"What will happen when we get to New York?" Carrie asked him. "Victor is dead, not that you would be going back to work for him anyway. Will you be able to gather your belongings?"

"I'm well acquainted with the staff of Mr. Anderson's home," he said with a nod. "It shouldn't be a problem."

"I'm sure that Mr. Ashton will be waiting at the dock for us. Jonathan can introduce you to him there. Perhaps you can arrange a meeting to discuss your blueprints."

Robert let out a sigh. "Thankfully, I have other drawings in my room back home. Otherwise, I'd have to start from scratch. I'll need to update them. Mr. Ashton will be so overjoyed to see the pair of you, I doubt he'll want to spend much time speaking to me."

"You'd be surprised. He's a kindhearted soul who also won't want to miss out on a possible business venture." Carrie gave him a reassuring smile.

"More importantly," Robert said, taking a deep breath, "I think we should discuss our situation."

Carrie swallowed hard, afraid he might say that things had changed between them. He had nearly died, after all, and while he'd been nothing but affectionate toward her, her pessimistic thoughts voiced their opinion that she shouldn't count her chickens prematurely. "Wh-what do we need to discuss?"

"Well, while I was lying in that hospital bed hoping you were alive but not knowing for certain, I thought a lot about what I want out of this second chance at life I've been given. It could have very easily been me lying on the dock amidst those corpses and not Victor."

Carrie nodded in understanding. "I'm so thankful all of us survived."

"Me, too. And Carrie, the only thing I could think about while I was recovering was seeing your smile again. One day in the hospital, I broke off the handle of my spoon."

Her eyebrows knit together. "Why would you do that?"

Without responding, he reached into the pocket of his second-hand jacket and pulled out a crudely shaped ring. "Well, because I don't have access to any of the money I've saved at the moment, but I told myself, as soon as I found you, I wanted to make this official–if you'll have me. But then, when I saw you, I was so overwhelmed. And then… the opportunity seemed to slip away. I've been thinking about it for the entire voyage but haven't had the courage to ask you. Until now."

With that, Robert stood and dropped to one knee. Tears sprang to Carrie's eyes as he reached for her left hand. "Carrie Boxhall, will you do me the honor of becoming my wife?"

Sobbing, Carrie couldn't do much more than nod. Eventually, she managed to choke out, "Yes! Yes, I will marry you, Robert Crawford."

He smiled as he brushed away his tears and pressed his lips to hers. "No matter where this life takes you, I want to be right by your side."

She laughed and pulled him into a tight hug. "I think my wander-lust has been sated, and I may never leave New York again, but I'll be perfectly content to spend the rest of my days right there in the city I love with the man I love.

They kissed again to seal the promise, and Carrie finally thought she could leave the terror of the disaster at sea behind her.

THE NEXT DAY, Robert carried her bag as they disembarked. Stepping onto the dock in New York harbor felt like coming home after years of wandering around lost in a foreign land. Mr. Ashton and Edward were there to greet them. When Jonathan embraced his partner unabashedly, Carrie smiled with pride. No one seemed to notice, but even if they did, she'd dare them to say something.

"Carrie! Thank the Lord above. I'm so happy to see you!" Mr. Ashton squeezed her so tightly she thought she might burst. "We're so grateful you're home safe and sound."

"I'm very happy to see you as well, Mr. Ashton. How is Mrs. Ashton?" she asked as soon as she could breathe again.

"She's doing quite well, thank you. Meg is at home with Henry and our baby girl, Johanna, named after my father and our friend Jonathan here." Pride was evident in every word Charlie spoke, his chest puffed out as he tugged at his lapels.

"A baby girl!" Carrie gushed. "How wonderful."

"Yes, we are pleased as punch. And who might this be? Don't tell me—Robert?" Charlie extended a hand to the man who'd been standing quietly behind Carrie.

"Yes, pardon my manners," Jonathan said, blushing a bit from his interaction with Edward and knowing that his friends had named their daughter after him. "This is Robert. We found him aboard the *St. Louis.*"

"Remarkable!" Charlie pounded Robert on the back. "Jonathan had sent me a telegram to let me know they were choosing to delay their return in looking for you. We've been praying you'd turn up. I'm so sorry about Mr. Anderson."

Carrie bit back a negative comment. No reason to speak ill of the dead. "Finding Robert was certainly an answered prayer," she said instead. Extending her hand, she said, "And we'll be getting married soon."

Charlie's eyes bulged. "Wonderful news! Meg will be thrilled for you, Carrie, though she'll hate losing your service. Never mind now. Let's get you back to the house to rest and see the baby."

"I believe I should head to Mr. Anderson's house to gather my belongings. Perhaps I could come by later?" Robert said.

"Anytime, anytime!" Charlie clapped him on the back again. "Let me get you a car."

"Oh, that's not necessary," Robert said, but Carrie interrupted.

"Actually, it is, dear. You lost all of your money on *Lusitania*, remember?" She smiled prettily at him.

"It's no trouble," Charlie insisted before Robert could try another way to get out of accepting Charlie's offer. Mr. Ashton signaled to one of the dock workers who jumped to have the chance to assist the millionaire who was known to tip so well.

Robert walked with them to the car, and even though Carrie knew she'd see him again soon, tears filled her eyes. "I'll be by directly," he told her.

"I know. Be careful, though. Don't get run over or find yourself at the mercy of a distracted driver."

He chuckled. "I'll be just fine." He kissed her cheek, and Carrie wanted more, but polite society dictated she accept the small token of affection.

With Robert on his way to take the car Charlie arranged for, she slipped in the backseat with Edward and Jonathan, leaving the front for Mr. Ashton, and his driver, Bix, headed home.

The streets of New York went by in a blur. Carrie watched the tall buildings and thanked God that she was home. She marveled at architectural features she'd never noticed before and wondered if she and Robert might make their home in one of the mansions they passed someday.

When they reached the Ashton home, they piled out. She took her bag from Jonathan and fished out the package she needed to give to Mrs. Ashton. While it had been tempting to open it on the boat, she hadn't done so since its contents were none of her business. Still, she was curious to see what Mildred Westmoreland had found so important. What was it she'd risked her life to retrieve?

In the house, she found Mrs. Ashton holding her bundle of joy in her arms in the parlor by a large window. Henry, Ruth, and Lizzie played nearby under the watchful eye of Mrs. Pendleton while their parents chatted on the sofa.

As soon as Mrs. Ashton saw Carrie and Jonathan, she rushed over, despite the baby and the fact that she'd only given birth a few days earlier. "Thank goodness!" she exclaimed as she wrapped an arm around Carrie. "We were so worried."

"I'm fine, just fine," Carrie assured her, even though she still wasn't sure that was true. "Let me see this beautiful girl."

Johanna's eyes were a beautiful blue, like her father's, and the soft downy hair on the top of her head was the same golden blonde as her mother's. She looked like a little angel, and seeing her almost made Carrie cry.

"Would you like to hold her?" Mrs. Ashton offered.

Carrie nodded and took the bundle in her arms. Johanna cooed and stuffed her little fist in her mouth. A silent prayer went up in that moment that someday Carrie would have a little girl who was the perfect blend of her and Robert.

"They found Robert," Mr. Ashton exclaimed. "He'll be over to visit soon."

"Wonderful!" Mrs. Ashton patted her arm. "I'm so glad to hear it."

"And what is that on your hand?" Kelly asked.

Remembering her ring, Carrie felt her cheeks flush. "Oh, we're getting married!"

Both of the other women let out a gasp of shock and joy. "Congratulations!" Mrs. Ashton hugged her again.

They took a few moments to get situated, and then, while Jonathan held his namesake, Carrie handed Mrs. Ashton the package.

She didn't open it right away. Instead, she placed it on her lap and pressed a palm to it, her eyes closed, as if she were saying a prayer. Carrie assumed she was simply composing herself.

When she finally opened it, she did so slowly, meticulously. The anticipation was killing Carrie as she wondered if it was all about to be worth it.

The first item she removed was a pocket watch. Instantly, tears filled Mrs. Ashton's eyes. Her husband sat next to her and wrapped an arm around her shoulders as she examined it. "I remember this," she said through her tears. "He'd check the time and say, 'Oh, yes! It's time for my hug!' and I'd run over and throw my arms around him." She took a quiet moment before she added, "I'd forgotten."

No one said anything, only gave her time to process.

Next, Meg pulled out a framed picture. It was her and her father.

Carrie would recognize that smile anywhere, and even though it was in black and white, she could tell the ringlets framing the girl's face were the same golden silk piled atop her head now. Mr. Westmoreland beamed at the camera, his arm wrapped around his little girl who had to have been about four. Meg sat on a chair in a fancy frock, smiling with glee and a hint of mischief.

"I see where Henry gets his smile now," Charlie joked. That got a chuckle out of everyone, even Meg whose tears continued to fall.

The last item she pulled from the envelope was a letter. She took a deep breath and scooted back on the couch slightly before opening it. The envelope was addressed to her.

Meg didn't read it aloud, but by the time she finished, she was openly weeping. Charlie handed her a handkerchief, and she dabbed her eyes, careful not to wet the paper.

"He… he said he loved me more than anything, that he was so proud of me, and he hoped I grew up to be the same sort of woman I was as a little girl–full of wonder and spirit. It's clear from the letter that he knew he was dying. I'm so thankful he managed to write his thoughts to me before… before…." She couldn't finish the sentence before she burst into tears and Mr. Ashton wrapped her up in a tight hug, but it wasn't necessary. Everyone knew how tragic the passing of Henry Westmoreland had been.

After taking a few moments to compose herself, Meg reached over to take Carrie's hand. "Thank you so much for all the trouble you went to." She looked at Jonathan. "Both of you. If I had known the danger you would've been in, I never would've asked you to go."

"I know that," Carrie assured her. "But if this helps you to gain some closure about your father's untimely departure, then believe me, it was all worth it. Besides, if we hadn't gone, I might never have become reacquainted with Robert."

Meg pulled Carrie into a tight embrace. "Thank you for being such a wonderful friend to me all these years. To repay your kindness, Charlie and I would love to give you and Robert a splendid wedding. Whatever you've dreamed of, it shall be."

"I don't know what to say," Carrie exclaimed, hugging Meg even tighter. "It's been such a blessing to work for you. I knew the moment I met you, as frightened and out of place as you were that night after your voyage on *Carpathia* that you were a special lady, Mrs. Ashton. Over the years, you've proved it time and again." She looked into Mrs. Ashton's eyes. "Thank you–for everything."

With a kind smile, she replied, "Call me Meg."

EPILOGUE

"Ladies and gentleman, may I present to you, Mr. and Mrs. Robert Crawford! You may kiss the bride!"

The audience exploded in cheers and clapping as Robert lifted the long, white lacy veil that separated him from his bride and pressed his lips to hers. Carrie felt a flutter in her chest as her heart began to beat differently. Now, her heart would always beat in time with his.

With wide smiles on their faces, the two of them turned to face the crowd, and the cheering continued. Together, they walked hand-in-hand down the aisle of the massive historical church Carrie had chosen for their ceremony. She grasped a bouquet of white lilies in her free hand as she smiled at her friends and family. The Ashtons had paid for her family to travel to the city for the wedding, and her parents beamed at her from the front row where they sat right next to Charlie, Meg, Henry, Johanna, Jonathan, and Edward. On the other side, her new family, Robert's family, grinned at them as well.

They made their way down the aisle with joy bubbling up in their chests. Once they were through the doors, they took a moment to kiss again. "I can't believe you're my wife," Robert whispered. Soon enough, they'd be waiting for their guests to filter by and tell them congratulations before heading off to have their portrait made and then take part in a reception so grand Carrie couldn't bring herself to look at the final bill. Charlie had said not to worry about it, so she was trying her best not to.

Not that Robert couldn't afford to pay for it himself now. In the six months since they'd returned from their journey, he'd taken a lucrative position in one of Charlie's companies, and the two of them had worked together to get his motorcoach patent accepted. Now, Charlie owned a new company which was working with motorcoach manufacturers to implement Robert's new technology, and he had already made over a hundred thousand dollars from the royalties alone. After their honeymoon in Upstate New York, they'd be moving into a grand home a few blocks away from Meg and Charlie. Carrie was so proud of everything he'd accomplished. That wasn't all he had in mind, though, and she loved chatting with him over tea about his other ideas. It was quite clear Robert Crawford was a talented, ambitious man who was on his way to improving their world in ways she couldn't even comprehend.

"I love you so much," he whispered as the first guests reached them.

"I love you, too."

"I'm so proud of you. My *petite modiste*."

Carrie couldn't help but laugh as Meg wrapped her in a tight hug and congratulated her. Robert had taken to calling her that since she opened her first dress shop a few months ago. She was hardly a *modiste*, but with Meg's influence, many of New York's most prominent women requested designer gowns regularly. Carrie had designed several that had quickly become the talk of the town and the hit of the season. Her heart swelled with overwhelming pride and love.

"Congratulations," Charlie told her, hugging her tightly. "I'm so proud of you, Carrie."

"Thank you, Mr.--Charlie." Old habits died hard. Sometimes, she still wanted to call them Mr. and Mrs. Ashton. He chuckled and pounded Robert on the back hardily.

When Jonathan reached her, Carrie felt the sting of tears in her eyes. She'd always been fond of the liegeman, but now, the two of them shared a bond no one else would ever understand. He was like a brother to her, and she couldn't wait to have children of her own for him to toss in the air and tickle until they squealed with laughter.

"Well done, Carrie," he whispered as they embraced. "I'm so happy for you."

"Thank you, my friend." It was hard to let him go when he'd been her lifeline for so long, but she knew that Robert would always be there for her. With a deep breath, she released the man who had saved her life and locked eyes with the man who had her heart.

The reception was wonderful, with tasty food and exquisite decorations. Carrie didn't have much time to take it all in. Everything happened so quickly, she hardly had time to taste the cake or smell the flowers.

But before they left to catch a private car to Niagara Falls, Carrie found herself wrapped up in Robert's arms once more for one last dance on their wedding day. It wouldn't be the last time she danced with her wonderful husband, though. Every chance she got for however many years she was blessed to spend with him, she'd take his hand and let him lead her out on the dance floor. When she closed her eyes, she saw a field of stars above her and heard the sweet refrain of Gretchen Flynn's voice as she sang a love song.

Not all of Carrie's memories of *Lusitania* were tragic.

"What are you thinking about, my love?" Robert whispered.

Carrie opened her eyes and stared into his dark orbs. "I was thinking… I'm so blessed to be your wife. And… I want to have a little boy with eyes just like yours."

A chuckle escaped Robert's lips. "I think we should get started on that right away. Now, if you're ready, let's start our next adventure."

Carrie smiled back. "As long as it doesn't involve a boat, I'm game."

Hand-in-hand, they set off together to start their next journey confident that they could survive anything as long as they were together.

A NOTE FROM THE AUTHOR

Thank you for reading Lusitania! I hope you enjoyed it. I hadn't intended to write another book in this series, but then I got the idea to write a book about Carrie and decided, "Why not?"

If you'd like to see another book, perhaps one about Britanic, please let me know! Please mention it in your review of Lusitania. If enough people are interested, I will write one! And I'll put it on preorder for 99 cents like this one was!

If you'd like to stay in touch, please sign up for my newsletter here:

https://books.bookfunnel.com/idjohnsonnewslettersignup

Please check out the rest of my books in the Also by ID Johnson page and check out my publisher's website where you can get several books for free at www.roguewolfpublishing.com

Thank you!

Immy

Realm Jumper

Celestial Springs

(psychological thriller/literary fiction/women's fiction)

<u>Beneath the Inconstant Moon</u>

<u>The First Mrs. Edwards</u>

<u>Leaving Ginny</u>

The Motherhood

(dystopian romance)

<u>Rain's Rebellion</u>

<u>Rain's Run</u>

<u>Rain's Return</u>

Ashes and Rose Petals

(contemporary romance/retelling of Romeo and Juliet and Cinderella)

<u>Girl in the Attic</u>

<u>Girl From the Tomb</u>

<u>Girl On the Beach</u>

Nashville Country Dreams

(contemporary romance)

<u>Meant to Marry Me</u>

<u>Lead Me Home</u>

<u>You Are the Reason</u>

Forever Love series

(clean romance/historical)

<u>Cordia's Will: A Civil War Story of Love and Loss</u>

<u>Cordia's Hope: A Story of Love on the Frontier</u>

The Clandestine Saga series

(paranormal romance)

Transformation

Resurrection

Repercussion

Absolution

Illumination

Destruction

Annihilation

Obliteration

Termination

A Vampire Hunter's Tale (based on The Clandestine Saga)

(paranormal/alternate history)

Aaron

Jamie

Elliott

Christian

The Chronicles of Cassidy (based on The Clandestine Saga)

(young adult paranormal)

So You Think Your Sister's a Vampire Hunter?

Who Wants to Be a Vampire Hunter?

How Not to Be a Vampire Hunter

My Life As a Teenage Vampire Hunter

Vampire Hunting Isn't for Morons

Vampires Bite and Other Life Lessons

Gone Guardian

Death Does Not Become Her

Blood of the Vampire Hunter (based on The Clandestine Saga)

(paranormal romance)

<u>Night Slayer</u>

<u>Shadow Stalker</u>

<u>Queen Catcher</u>

<u>Mother Hunter</u>

<u>Father Finder</u>

Ghosts of Southampton series

(historical romance)

<u>Prelude</u>

<u>Titanic</u>

<u>Residuum</u>

<u>Lusitania</u>

Heartwarming Holidays Sweet Romance series

(Christian/clean romance)

<u>Melody's Christmas</u>

<u>Christmas Cocoa</u>

<u>Winter Woods</u>

<u>Waiting On Love</u>

<u>Shamrock Hearts</u>

<u>A Blossoming Spring Romance</u>

<u>Firecracker!</u>

<u>Falling in Love</u>

<u>Thankful for You</u>

<u>Melody's Christmas Wedding</u>

<u>The New Year's Date</u>

Charles Town Brides (based on Heartwarming Holidays Sweet Romance)

(Christian/clean romance)

<u>From This Moment</u>

Can't Help Falling in Love

It's Your Love

When You Say Nothing At All

My Girl

Unchained Melody

I Only Have Eyes For You

At Last

The Very Thought of You

Reaper's Hollow

(paranormal/urban fantasy)

Ruin's Lot

Ruin's Promise

Ruin's Legacy

When Kings Collide

(steamy historical romance)

Princess of Silence

Princess of Hearts

Collections

Ghosts of Southampton Books 0-2

Reaper's Hollow Books 1-3

The Clandestine Saga Books 1-3

The Chronicles of Cassidy Books 1-4

Celestial Springs Collection

Heartwarming Holidays Sweet Romance Books 1-3

Heartwarming Holidays Sweet Romance Books 4-7

Websites: https://books2read.com/ap/xX7ZD8/ID-Johnson

For updates, visit www.authoridjohnson.blogspot.com

Follow on Twitter @authoridjohnson

Find me on Facebook at www.facebook.com/IDJohnsonAuthor

Instagram: @authoridjohnson

Follow me on Bookbub: https://www.bookbub.com/authors/id-johnson